Letters to London

September 1860 – January 1863

David Powell

Edwalton Press

First published in Great Britain 2000
by Edwalton Press
Peterborough PE3 6ER

British Library Cataloguing-in-Publication Data.
A catalogue record for this book is available from the British Library.

Cover design by Nick Bartlett
Designed and typeset by Curran Publishing Services Ltd, Norwich
Printed and bound in England by
Barnwell's Print Ltd., Aylsham, Norfolk NR11 6ET

ISBN 0-9538965-0-1

Prologue

This book is about the views of a young man in the mid-1800s, which are expressed through his letters. The story is fiction, but it should be noted that fiction is born out of facts.

The story starts when Mrs Grenville presents her husband with a son, Richard, in the early hours of 29th May 1836, at their moderate estate situated in East Anglia. Richard's childhood is spent within the confines of the estate. Great fuss, concern and attention is lavished on the boy by his parents, since he is their only child and heir. This quiet lifestyle causes young Richard to withdraw into himself, and acquire little interest in conversing. Life for him, after his daily lessons with a tutor, is to wander alone within the boundaries of the estate, where Mother Nature becomes his friend and companion.

In his puberty he encounters distractions in the form of females. He learns of their wiles, and also gains an understanding of female emotions. Naturally he experiences bodily urges, and partakes of carnal knowledge with a number of the maids.

This tranquil pleasant life ceases in 1857 when he is sent to join his uncle's business in London. It is a dramatic change from his life on the estate. Throughout his time in London he is unable to adjust to the alien environment. Consequently he works long hours, seven days a week, in his uncle's office, and every night goes directly to his nearby lodgings, from where he does not stir until it is time to rise and briskly walk to the office. He is anxious not to become embroiled in the sins of the city, or play a part in its bawdiness and crimes. His apparent dedication and punctilious efforts are noticed by his uncle, who decides to entrust his nephew with a momentous venture for the company.

In 1860 Richard Grenville, now a young man, prepares to embark on the journey of a lifetime. He sits in his lodgings to collect his emotions and thoughts before he writes to his father and mother. His correspondence is presented here for perusal, and to invite you to accompany him on that journey through his 'Letters to London'.

London
2 September 1860

Dear father,

I trust you are well and all is satisfactory with the estate. My reason for writing is to inform you that Uncle Silas has bestowed on me the honour of representing the company in America. Regretfully I must be brief, as there is much to do to prepare for my journey if I am to arrive in Portsmouth on the fourteenth. My uncle is anxious I waste no time and has secured a berth on the 'Sea Hawk' which sails on the sixteenth. Its being a trading vessel means I do not expect to disembark in New York until the twenty-fourth, subject to fair winds.

On American soil I shall be responsible for my well-being and comforts, as my uncle will not be in a position to assist me, due to distance and time. I do not know what will befall me on this venture, or its duration, and do ask your forgiveness if I am lax in writing to you.

May I humbly suggest you seek news of my progress from Uncle Silas to whom I shall correspond regularly regarding the venture.

I remain, as ever, your obedient son. . .

London
2 September 1860

My dearest mother,

I trust you are in good health and all is well with you. Please do not be alarmed, or worry about me, when I tell you Uncle Silas has honoured me, and the family, with an extraordinarily important venture on behalf of the company. The venture is to represent the company in America. Because I know how you dislike details, and I do not wish to distress you, I have written to father with the information of my departure from England, and my arrival in America. Uncle Silas does not waste time, so it is no surprise that I expect to disembark in New York on the twenty-fourth. The thought of this venture fills me with numerous emotions. I am apprehensive because of the unknown, yet excited by the challenge presented to me.

My immediate problem is what to expect on my landfall. It is said the land is of gigantic portions and England fits within it many times over. I find this hard to visualize. In addition to the numerous races who have settled there, I anticipate meeting the native tribes who have dwelled on the land since before the first explorers arrived. It is my hope I shall learn of their cultures.

Dear mother, please do not fear for me whilst I am in America, and promise to be vigilant at all times, so that I may return to the bosom of the family when the venture is completed.

I remain for ever, your loving son. . .

One
The volcano

New York
30 September 1860

Sir,

I have the pleasure to inform you of my arrival seven days ago in the coastal port of New York.

During my uneventful voyage I struck up an acquaintance with a fellow passenger who is knowledgeable about this continent. Indeed, in addition to the information imparted, he was agreeably helpful in recommending an establishment where I may stay during my visit, which lodgings I can report are most satisfactory. The matron is well proportioned and extremely pleasant by nature. She is excellently versed with her gentlemen's needs. The establishment serves me well, its location being especially satisfactory for my explorations.

My impressions, based on my preliminary investigations, are that the town has a busy and thriving centre for trade of imports and, to a lesser degree, exports. I have been able to ascertain that the dock facilities and warehousing are ample and adequate for our requirements, and therefore anticipate no problem should the Board wish to consider appropriate action after my detailed report. This I anticipate will be dispatched within seven days.

Apart from the docklands, my remaining time to date has been employed within the town's central area where there are three main functions. The first is commerce, in substantial evidence; the second is pursuing trade with the local populace; the third is concerned with property to accommodate the townspeople. The main building material appears to be timber, of which I am given to understand there is an abundance inland.

From numerous conversations with people I was further able to ascertain that it is in the suburbs that the wealthy and influential citizens are to be found. In addition, much of the industry is in outlying areas. I intend to devote the forthcoming days to such areas to ascertain the validity of my information.

The town is cosmopolitan, and yet I detect an excited, controlled anticipation no matter where I went and with whom I conversed. I would respectfully equate it to that experienced by the populace when our gracious monarch Queen Victoria was crowned. There is a sense of a second, as yet submerged element, and I would liken it to a great event of history, about to explode on the country, and be of greater devastation than that attributed to the eruption of a volcano. What it is, and how it may affect my mission, I am at present unsure, but I intend to pursue my inquiries with the utmost vigour.

My letter is brief, to enable you to present the Board with a preliminary report of my initial observations. In particular, may I respectfully request you include the following when you report to the Board: that one subject on which all here seem to be agreed is that this land is one that offers many and great opportunities for the stout-hearted.

I am, and remain, your obedient servant. . .

Washington
7 November 1860

Sir,

Events have brought me post-haste to the capital, for it is here I will obtain information of great import.

This letter will be in two parts: the first part for the Board, the second privy for you.

Regarding the Board's report: my impression, based on brief research, suggests New York has well-established commerce and trading organizations. I would therefore respectfully recommend to you and the Board that it would not be in the interests of the company to compete in these areas. There are, however, other areas where as yet demands have not been exploited to full potential; I refer to the wealthy and influential class.

The country boasts immense ranges of raw materials including timber, iron, coal, copper, gold and silver. My survey indicates few skilled tradespeople currently practising in New York, and the organization of those few is haphazard in the extreme. Further, I suggest that British products would help to provide additional comforts for the populace. A majority of the inhabitants of New York still retain links with us and the continent of

Europe; I feel many would applaud an enterprise that created greater access to European fashions.

Sir, I do strongly recommend a representative of the company be dispatched immediately to New York with the prime objective of identifying specific areas from which the company will benefit greatly. In addition, a native of New York should be recruited to assist in the enterprise. The establishment of an office will be no problem: the citizens are more than capable of striking a bargain.

However, I must sound one warning. The wealthy and influential in the area are frugal gentlefolk, and to a lesser degree this also applies to the lower classes of the society. The many different racial groups living in New York far exceed those of London in every respect, therefore confrontations and conflicts occur with alarming frequency. I am given to understand that the law and judiciary take a lenient attitude to the outbursts; their view appears to be that strong enforcement is undesirable as this may well fan the bitterness still simmering below the surface of many who fled the repression and persecutions of their home lands.

Touching on the subject of religion, I discovered an avid evangelist movement whose followers come mainly from among the younger emigrés. I had an opportunity to converse with several, and all generally agreed they found the ideas exciting and fresh after the political restrictions and religious tyranny of their native lands.

Even though my stay in New York was brief I did have the opportunity to devote several hours to the study of maps whose accuracy has been enhanced through recent vigorous surveys. The people of this land have developed an effective waterway system, utilizing many of the rivers that traverse this continent. I have also had the good fortune to experience first-hand their railroad system during my travel from New York to Washington. The various classes of carriage differed little: all tend to be primitive, devoid of luxury, and lacking comfort, which would prove extremely inconvenient for journeys lasting several days.

One of the passengers did relate to me an amusing tale of a certain personage who had his own carriage designed and built to his specification; this person would then arrange with the railroad to attach his carriage to the appropriate train heading in the desired direction, so you will see that the land is indeed ripe with enterprise.

The railroad system is extensive and relates to the vastness of the land. It also has telegraphic communication along the various routes, and the advantage of this will be obvious to you.

Sir, I respectfully submit this report to you and the honourable members of the Board for due deliberation.

With your permission I would convey to you certain events of history that may well have a bearing on my mission to this land and its successful conclusion. I would however, respectfully request that the contents be for your eyes only.

Since our forefathers set down on this land, democracy has diverged from that in the United Kingdom. In the past decade, there has been a gradual process of the individual states joining under a single national government in Washington, which process continues to the present day. Each state joining has been able to stipulate its terms for membership, thus retaining a degree of self-government. However, I understand that in recent years there has been discontent on the part of some southern states as to the fairness of the Washington government. These states feel aggrieved and at a disadvantage compared to those in the north.

The controlled anticipation I referred to earlier has been explained since my coming into the capital: namely, I have arrived in the midst of an election, concluded yesterday, 6th November, for a president of the United States. The present incumbent, President Buchanan, will relinquish office in March of next year.

This morning I awoke to learn the president-elect is a gentleman by the name of Abraham Lincoln who hails from Illinois. I know nothing of him, and on questioning those about me have come to the conclusion most people know little of the gentleman himself but a great deal of his politics.

It is necessary for me to seek information and explanations of the essential circumstances of this year before a decision can be reached regarding the pursuit of the enterprise and its direction. Sir, I hopefully anticipate your approval to cease pursuance of the company's enterprise until I have relevant details of this past year, without which I fear it may be detrimental for the company to proceed at this time beyond the steps which I proposed for New York.

There is an atmosphere of uncertainty within the United States and I need to seek clarity. I sense the past holds the clues to the future; the volcano's eruption may be imminent.

I am, and remain, your obedient servant. . .

Washington
20 December 1860

Sir,

I am pleased to inform you I am in a position to convey the information I have been seeking.

The seed was, paradoxically, sown when states first joined the Union of States. At that time opponents to the process of union were ineffectual, their objections seeming to have been based on the subject of trade. The abundant raw materials of the southern states were to be sold to the industrial northern states who in turn would manufacture products for which the southern states paid a high price.

Be it through apathy, ignorance, or the confidence of Union supporters in the future, the anti-Unionists failed to win the day. However, there has been a change of mood in certain states. The anti-Unionists have become secessionists with a reasonable following, but the greater number of the populace is undecided. The mention of war is a remarkable deterrent. The opinion of most is that the secessionists are hotheads. They, who are in the majority, feel that all matters can be resolved and desire the Union to continue.

Democrats were the first to set the scene with their convention in Charleston, a predominantly secessionist area. At the opening gavel in April of this year, the southern Democrats demanded that that the northern Democrats support a federal slave code that would protect the rights of slaveholders anywhere in the Union. Stalemate. They tried again in June in Baltimore; again a split. This time Stephen Douglas gained a nomination from one section of the party. The southern delegates sought John Breckinridge as their candidate. Then a further split occurred when a faction elected John Bell as their candidate.

There was now a confusing situation. Breckinridge stood for the federal slave code, Douglas to confine slavery. Bell stood for the constitution, the Union, and enforcement of laws. I understand deals were struck in order to find a compromise; however, one of the three reneged. Thus there were three candidates to oppose the Republicans.

The Republicans adopted a something-for-all stand. The contest was between William Seward and Abraham Lincoln. Lincoln's supporters won the nomination through management and striking bargains. The conclusion was dramatic, when an Ohio delegate switched four votes to Lincoln. From all the information I have available, it would seem a foregone conclusion that Abraham Lincoln will be elected the next president. The party draws support from the north and the west, where much of the food is grown, industry is strong and the population large, and this could be sufficient without any support from the southern states.

Strangely, the election itself did not focus on the slavery problem as being the key issue. For reasons beyond my comprehension, the debate and arguments revolved around the future of the Union. From public sources I learned there have been considerable efforts by various senators with proposals to resolve certain delicate issues. These have been defeated or rejected in the Senate.

This day, 20th December, I actually sensed the volcano rumbling. Sir, you will appreciate events are proceeding at a headlong pace and I fear disaster is nigh. I will therefore send this letter without further delay to enable you to have full knowledge of events to date. The future of the company's enterprise and its direction can be determined once the play has reached its conclusion.

I am, and remain, your obedient servant. . .

Richmond
2 February 1861

Sir,

I considered it expedient to travel the short distance from the Union capital to Richmond, which to all intents and purposes has become the centre of a proposed new Confederation.

Since my last letter, I have been exceedingly busy documenting the rapid events that have led to this present state of affairs. There is a strong undercurrent, led by agitators and orators of great persuasion, seeking a force of arms against what is left of the Union. These people argue that the Confederacy would continue to be dominated by the northern states, since they are predominant in matters of trade and commerce. Such stifling control imposed from the north would be intolerable to the people of the south; thus the influence must be destroyed.

Many politicians, on both sides, and of all political persuasions, are earnestly seeking a peaceful compromise to avert the dreadful and unthinkable prospect of war. However I run ahead of myself. For the sake of clarity I shall present you with a chronological catalogue of events to date.

On the morning of 21st December 1860 I awoke to find much agitation among the people of Washington. Some were in a state of shock, others in disbelief, and still others in jubilant and jocular mood. The source of the excitement was the news that South Carolina had actually committed the act of secession the previous day in the port of Charleston. I overheard one such person with Confederate leanings, boldly state: 'North and South are finally divorced. Praise be. There was never any love between them, only hate.'

There followed days of rumours. It was also generally agreed there was uncertainty about South Carolina's intent. One such persistent rumour related to three forts, the custodians of Charleston, which are at present still occupied by the Union military. South Carolina demanded their surrender, and claimed an act of aggression had been committed by the newly arrived fort commander, when on the 27th December Major Robert Anderson did concentrate all his command within the walls of Fort Sumpter.

The Major had been appointed because he was from Kentucky, therefore presumably with a southern bias, while the secretary for war, John B. Floyd, was himself a Virginian and responsible for the appointment of Major Anderson. A South Carolina delegation journeyed to Washington seeking the surrender of the fort, prepared to purchase it if need be. Things became unclear at that time. President Buchanan prevaricated in the hope that the matter could wait until March. The cabinet was said to be in a state of chaos with no decision forthcoming; Mr Floyd and Mr Thompson departed from the cabinet.

The South Carolina delegation left on 30th December, after the President had finally rejected their request. An ominous date indeed. What would 1861 bring? Rumours once more abounded regarding the fate of Fort Sumpter; taverns and public places hummed with theories and schemes. Not until 10th January of this year did news reach me that at 6 o'clock the previous morning, the *Star of the West* had been fired upon as it attempted to land supplies and reinforcements at Fort Sumpter.

I truly expected to find the volcano had finally erupted. But no, it had not. The press of both regions however, did erupt in a series of angry exchanges and abuses. No one in a position of authority seemed prepared to claim the honour of starting the war. I sensed extreme reluctance on the part of every man, woman and child to embark on that slippery slope, into the abyss of torment, despair, sorrow and misery.

Thereafter matters deteriorated rapidly. The state of Mississippi seceded on 9th January, followed by Florida on the 10th, Alabama on the 11th, Georgia on the 19th, Louisiana on the 26th and Texas on 1st February. These states acted quickly against Union establishments. On 12th January the state of Florida attempted to seize two forts. On 20th January a Union port facility was occupied by the state of Mississippi. This was followed on the 24th with news that the state of Georgia had taken an arsenal and fort, whilst the state of Louisiana controlled military installations. The final blow fell in the state of Texas, when the top Union officer, Major General Twiggs, surrendered the military posts under his command.

Sir, I fear the seeds of destruction have been sown. All must now wait for the spark that must truly and inevitably come to this land, though from whence it will come is uncertain. The business of forming a government seems now to be of paramount importance. The seven states which have seceded are inviting the states of Arkansas, Delaware, Kentucky, Maryland, North Carolina, Tennessee and Virginia to secede and join the Confederacy.

Sir, I would advise you that in the time available I propose to use the railroad to assess the Confederacy as regards the company's enterprise. My intention is to leave tomorrow, and at an indeterminate date, return to Richmond having accomplished my mission.

I am, and remain, your obedient servant. . .

Two
Into the abyss

Richmond
5 March 1861

Sir,

I have safely arrived this very afternoon, and feel I should put pen to paper to record my immediate thoughts.

Indeed, the progress of this land seems to be rushing on apace; I feel sure it will take me an extraordinary length of time to adjust from my accustomed English view, that history is sedate. The first matter of importance is the map of this land. Might I therefore humbly recommend the map held by the company be modified. This will assist you and the Board when receiving my letters.

Since I left Richmond on 2nd February, events have created much change; ideals have solidified. Prior to 1861, a portion of the country existed as territories which had not advanced into statehood. These are known by the name of Kansas, Nebraska, New Mexico, Utah and Washington. These areas, I have been informed, are interested in joining the present fragmented Union. Majorities in each are opposed to slavery. Those seeking to extend slavery produce a blustering facade which is in general ignored.

The remaining two territories have the quaint title of Unorganised. The turmoil within the territories does not touch upon the two Unorganised Territories. Presumably, those who inhabit the areas are mainly natives of the type originally encountered by the Pilgrim Fathers. It is sad to know that these peoples have been confined so. I am informed they are know as Red Indians, or by the less complimentary title of Redskin, the red derived from initial encounters and impressions. Their skins are in fact brown, yet bear a resemblance to the soil which is of a reddish colour. Time permitting, it might be possible to visit these peoples with a view to trade or barter.

The political structure is unique, the like of which I have not previously encountered. A state may negotiate its terms for entry into the Union. This I fear is the weakness in the system, as is presently demonstrated, since it is also possible for a state to secede. The debate rages as to the legality of this act.

States presently within the Union are California, Connecticut, Illinois, Indiana, Iowa, Maine, Massachusetts, Michigan, Minnesota, New Hampshire, New Jersey, New York, Ohio, Oregon, Pennsylvania, Rhode Island, Vermont and Wisconsin. The states of Delaware and Maryland are undecided; the general consensus of opinion is that these two will remain within the Union.

Pray sir, do not be misled into believing that the vastness of territory is reflected by the number of states: there are some which compare in area to that of the United Kingdom.

At present the following states have formed themselves into a Confederacy: Alabama, Florida, Georgia, Louisiana, Mississippi, South Carolina and Texas. It is likely the slave states of Arkansas, North Carolina, Tennessee and Virginia will also secede to join them.

The remaining slave states of Kentucky and Missouri may stay in the Union for economic reasons. The majority of the Union states appear tolerant of the situation, which does not directly contravene the official policy. Indeed, many hope by example to encourage the ultimate abolition of slavery in the two states concerned.

That, sir, is the present state of affairs at this time of writing: the Confederated states desire to be recognized by, and to trade with, the world, while the Union states hold the view that it is undesirable to divide, as this leads to weakness. Thus, sir, time should tell whether battle or trading-lines have been drawn.

Sir, please excuse me; I am unable to continue due to exhaustion brought about by my lengthy excursions into the southern lands. When I next write, I shall do so at length, to explain my reasons for the undertaking, my conclusions, and recommendations.

Should you, sir, and the honourable gentlemen of the Board, approve any matters raised in my letters, I shall be only too happy to implement any specific wish, or instruction, with the utmost vigour. In the meantime I shall gather all the information available, here in Richmond, for that period of my absence. I am, and remain, your obedient servant. . .

Richmond
10 March 1861

Sir,

The newspapers in this land serve the public well. The reporting of the facts is accurate, due to the transcontinental communication system of the telegraph. However, the editors stamp their individual characters on the newspapers and have their own style of rhetoric that can truly stir a reader: many articles have been embellished with vivid descriptions and an occasional dramatic photograph. Little seems left for one's own imagination.

The geographics are now known to you and the honourable gentlemen of the Board. I feel it is also important to understand the peoples of this new and emerging land, with whom the company proposes to trade. It is one matter to know our European neighbours, but entirely another to know those people who have migrated and settled in this land. They are no longer subdued, but have thrown off their shackles. Their characters are undergoing an intrinsic change, confidence, astuteness and ambition rising to the surface, yet strangely they cling determinedly to their European cultures.

The matter I wrote of in my last letter of 5th March has taken another decisive step: I refer to the inauguration of the sixteenth President of the Union, Mr A. Lincoln, in Washington on 4th March. Prior to that date the Confederacy had chosen their first President, Mr J. Davis, whose inauguration took place in Montgomery on 18th February. I trust this will be an end to the matter and both will be able to mature to nationhood, in harmony, trade and mutual cooperation.

Now I will turn to the reason for my excursion. This was not embarked upon from idle curiosity, but to gain first-hand experience and information that would enhance the business prospects of the company.

Since my arrival on this continent, I have learned something of the northern states, the Union. The same cannot be said of the southern states, the Confederacy. My impression is that the Union was and still is the controlling influence, and that the northern states are also the more receptive to expansion and enterprise. Great and spectacular strides have been made during these past decades.

Although the southern states appear content with their accomplishments, they are nevertheless resentful of the trading conditions imposed by the northern states. Therefore, I felt it essential to survey the southern states, with a view to ascertaining future development prospects. It should be borne in mind that these states are about to set out as an independent trading group, and will need to develop and exploit their natural resources. These I was determined to discover.

I was also able to put to the test the railway system of the land. Thus, with the help of a few friends and contacts, I planned a route to take me through as many of the southern states as possible, starting from Richmond, thence through Bristol, Chattanooga, Memphis, running from east to west. The north-to-south route was from Memphis to Jackson and New Orleans, and from there by ship to Mobile to join the railway northwards to Montgomery, Columbus, Macon and Atlanta. I once again turned south to the infamous Charleston. Here, I again took ship along the coast, in an easterly and north direction, my destination being Wilmington. Finally I took train for the north to Richmond, passing through Petersburg en route.

My journey introduced me to many wonders of the land. Its names: English, European, and native, with their strange spellings; its countryside with the ever-changing panoramas; its people, especially those in communities created new upon virgin soil, yet retaining cultural habits. It was not difficult on occasion to identify the origins of such communities.

My other impression was how easy it is to be lost in such space. Peering out across the landscape, it was impossible to visualize thousands of homesteads, each isolated from their nearest neighbour by a hundred miles or more.

Sir, with your forbearance, I wish to record the discoveries that influenced my conclusions and thus, hopefully, enlighten you and the honourable gentlemen as to my perceptions. I wrote of my intention to seek the wealth of the Confederacy and this I have been able to ascertain. It comprises cattle, cotton, tobacco and agriculture. The area is served by the ports of New Orleans and Mobile on the southern-coast line, Charleston and Savannah on the eastern-coast line. Each port is reasonably close to the next, and each is well served by a railway that reaches most parts of the Confederacy. Goods can reach their destination within a week or less, once discharged from the vessels. The ports are adequate for establishing initial imports, though no doubt, through enterprise, the facilities could be enhanced for greater volumes.

The rivers are ideally placed to supplement the transportation network. However, twisting and meandering as they do, to use them would increase transportation times and costs. Nevertheless, these rivers do serve areas that the railway cannot.

The Mississippi is one such waterway that is presently exploited commercially and could easily afford access to many towns and communities along its banks.

Sir, and gentlemen, I must stress at this point, whether rail or waterway is selected, ultimately there will be portions of the route where goods would have to be conveyed by wagons, devices not encountered in the United Kingdom. Perhaps an adequate means of describing them would be to borrow the term used with endearment by the populace: the 'prairie schooner'. This indeed expresses their appearance and function. To assist you further, I have pleasure in enclosing an artist's sketch. Enclosed also is my sketch of the rail and waterway networks in the Confederacy.

A matter of importance I intend to pursue relates to land. My impression is that vast areas remain unclaimed. Whilst I investigate the legal situation, perhaps I may prevail upon you, sir, and the gentlemen of the Board, for permission to engage the services of a number of surveyors familiar with their own domains, to compile reports. This of course would be executed in a manner so as not to arouse suspicion of our true intent.

In conclusion, I have to report that time did not allow me to explore and detail the areas at each of the stops along the route. It was merely an exploratory exercise to establish the worth of a transportation network and the main economies of each state. Therefore I recommend that, once the present political tension has been resolved and a stable atmosphere prevails, I should conduct a further reconnaissance in greater depth and detail. My present intention is to study the policies that should emerge from the new presidencies, for which purpose it will be necessary to spend time in Washington and Richmond, therefore may I respectfully request your reply and instructions be directed to my Richmond establishment.

I trust my communications meet with your approval and are in accord with your wishes and the company's intentions.
I am, and remain, your obedient servant. . .

Richmond
24 March 1861

Sir,

This very day I have returned with joyful news. It would seem the lines to be drawn between Union and the Confederacy will, after all, be those of trade. I am especially pleased as this bodes

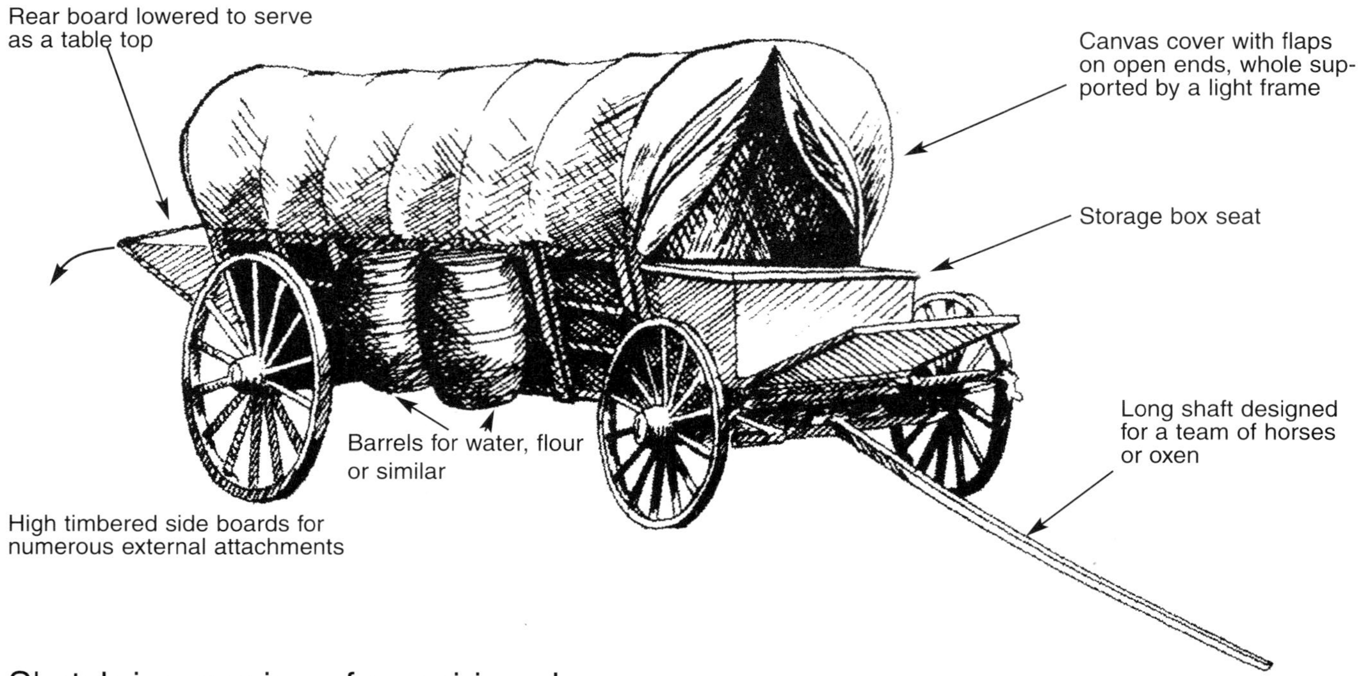

Sketch impression of a prairie schooner

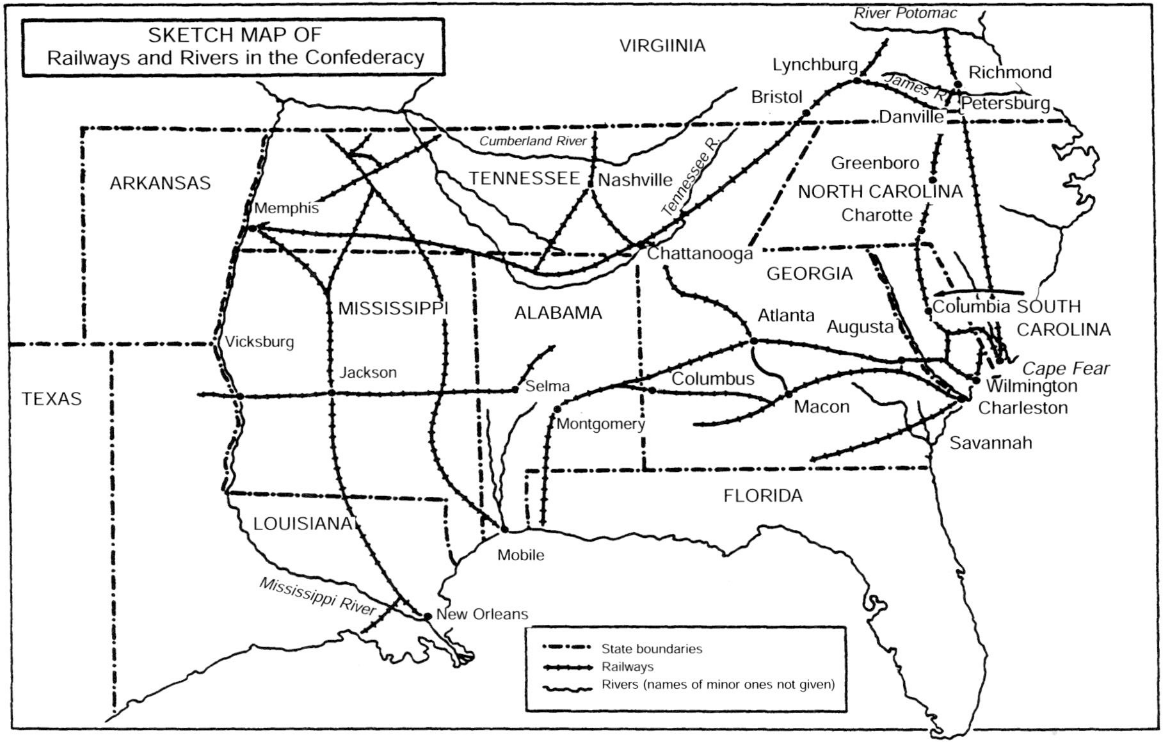

SKETCH MAP OF
Railways and Rivers in the Confederacy

well for the company's enterprise. With the threat of war now permanently removed, there should be no obstacle to activating a number of proposals at present before you and the gentlemen of the Board.

The last fourteen days have proved extremely productive, the time being spent obtaining drafts of the two President's speeches, which I will forward to you. However, I place before you in this letter the relevant extracts.

President Davis stated: 'All the Southerners want to be left alone, but if attacked, they will defend themselves. The suffering of millions will bear testimony to the folly and wickedness of our aggressors.'

President Lincoln vowed to avoid war and at the same time to maintain the Union. He held the Union is still whole, for it is by nature indissoluble. He would enforce the laws and hold, occupy, and possess Federal property. He would not initiate violent or aggressive action. He said: 'In your hands, my dissatisfied fellow-countrymen, and not in mine, is the momentous issue of civil war. You can have no conflict without yourselves the aggressors.' He had sworn to defend the Union, and would do so if necessary, but questioned that the Southerners would force his hand if they but took the time for reflection. 'We are not enemies, but friends. We must not be enemies.' Memories of the patriot days of the Revolution still bind all together. These fond sentiments will swell the chorus of the Union, when touched, as surely they will be, by the better angels of our nature.

While I was in Washington, the newspapers printed President Davis's speech without bias. They seemed to be expressing the thoughts of many northerners: let the seceded state have a peaceful separation. One statement supported by many was: 'Let the erring sisters go in peace.' President Lincoln appeared to have a firm grip of the situation. Any action on his part would be in accordance with his speech, yet any action actually undertaken could not be construed as provocative. He seemed desirous of seeking peaceable means to entice the errant states back into the Union fold.

Here in Richmond it is a little difficult to gauge the mood of the populace accurately. Some did breathe a sigh of relief, while others were outspoken about President Lincoln's speech. In their view it was ambiguous, vulgar and insolent. The minority is claiming that it is everywhere considered as a virtual declaration of war. This I am told is the usual outburst from the hotheads; it has all been heard before, when secessionists were in a minority. I believe this fraction carries little power, and does not reflect the mood of the masses, who generally remain quiet. A good sign methinks, that all will be resolved amicably, given time.

With prospects now brighter, I am confident of pursuing with the utmost intent the Company's enterprise. I therefore intend to visit New York to review my original assessment, and determine what action to recommend to you, sir, and the Board, thus enabling me thereafter to concentrate on the Confederacy.

I am, and remain, your obedient servant. . .

New York
6 April 1861

Sir,

I am now lodged with the good lady who provided me with accommodation when first I set foot in this town.

I have been able to complete my survey of the area, and have concluded there are opportunities for high-class trade, also ventures into the craft trades. When I first wrote to you, I proposed having an agent from England and one assistant, native to the area. I have conducted interviews of selected persons whom I consider well suited and qualified for the task. Enclosed with this letter are my reports of each interview so that you, sir, and the gentlemen of the Board may pass judgement.

Should you be persuaded to proceed with this enterprise and appoint an agent, then I feel sure the aforementioned reports will be of value to the agent. I must emphasize that at no time during the interviews did I indicate my purpose or implicate the name of the company, my subterfuge being that of a historian.

To make further progress, I now intend to engage a guide for a trip into the surrounding area, my prime intent being to note the prospects for the company. The journey will not involve railways. I will travel through the small state of New Jersey to arrive at Philadelphia, on the eastern boundary of Pennsylvania. From there I will travel to the River Potomac, to a small place known as Harper's Ferry, where an incident took place which was to be the first spark of the present turmoil. I shall then arrive in Washington, where I hope to write you of my observations.

I am, and remain, your obedient servant. . .

Charleston
14 April 1861

Sir,

I must apologize for writing from this unscheduled stop without advance communication.

Previously, I ventured to comment that history here was conducted at a giddy pace, and so it is at this significant moment in time. With difficulty I arrived here on the evening of the eleventh, having journeyed with a haste considered on my part to be imperative. The Company's enterprise might well have been in ruins, if a rumoured disaster had been proved true. But I run before myself. This letter must be in strict chronological sequence to convey my actions fully.

As stated in my previous letter, I did depart New York with my guide on the sixth, good fortune indeed. It was providence that I should have departed at that time for any delay, even a day or an hour, and I might not have witnessed this catastrophe.

The journey to Philadelphia was uneventful, speedy, and showed nothing likely to lead to the Company's gain, but some instinct was urging me forward, and therefore it was no surprise to arrive quite soon on the north bank of the River Potomac, across from Harper's Ferry.

On first sight the place appeared quiet and languid. This small, inauspicious hillside town of around fifty dwellings had its brief moment of notoriety on 16th October 1859. A certain personage by the name of John Brown had been mounting his personal campaign against slave-owners. He was a man of blood, yet known as 'The Avenging Angel', which title may have been gained through his religious fervour. He, accompanied by sixteen white men and five blacks, did cross the bridge and seize a federal armoury on the river bank. A great hue and cry went out the following morning. The authorities were so quick to react since they feared an uprising by the slaves, whom Brown intended to arm.

The military soon took command. Their commander was Lieutenant Colonel Robert E. Lee, and his aide Lieutenant James Ewell Brown.

Justice was executed with speed, and the man hanged on 2nd December.

It felt strange when standing on the north bank in this year of 1861, to be so aware of history. In 1859, both sides of the river were part of one Union, yet within the space of twelve months that picture would change. The north bank: Union soil; the south bank likely to be Confederate soil, separated by a short bridge supported by five pillars. Is not there a reference in the Bible to five pillars?

Yet another quirk of history: these townfolk were strongly Unionist, but lived on the wrong side of the river.

While at Harper's Ferry, I did strike up a conversation with a traveller recently come from Washington, who imparted to me a startling rumour. Rumour or truth, I needed to ascertain which at the earliest possible moment, hence my hasty departure from the place.

I arrived in the infamous Charleston on the evening of 11th April, a little before midnight, where my worst fears seemed confirmed. The town apparently was fully awake that night. An unmistakable excitement could be detected in most of the citizenry. Sleep was not in evidence at all, indeed the situation was growing in tension with every passing hour.

I understand that a surrender note had been delivered to the fort on the evening I arrived, from the Confederate commander, General Beauregard, to the Union commander, Major Anderson. There was extreme hesitancy on the part of the Confederate commander to be the first to fire, for numerous reasons. The hope was that a surrender could be achieved, thus averting war.

Another effort was made at one o'clock in the morning on 12th April. Major Anderson replied he was prepared to evacuate on the 15th, with provisos, which procrastination exasperated the Confederates. It is my sad duty to inform you that at 4.30 a.m. on 12th April, a Lieutenant Henry S. Farley was responsible for firing the signal shell to open the bombardment of the Union fort. Since then there has been a heavy cannonade from the Confederate guns and, to a lesser extent, from the fort. The noise has been deafening at times. During the night the sky looked like the Devil's inferno. From a vantage place I was able to discern five points where flashes were visible. Later I learned these missiles were being lobbed into the fort from distances of from 1,000 to 2,300 yards. It made me shudder to know death could be flung across such distances. If this is the face of war then it is both gruesome and fearsome to behold, yet I could not help but be fascinated by the spectacle.

First a spit of red fire, to be followed by a quiet whine and sometimes a whistle; then a crunch, and in the next instance a plume of smoke, the result of impact. It is truly remarkable that all this could be seen and heard at such a distance. Man's inventive ingenuity for destruction can be awesome, once released.

From military sources I understand that fifty-six guns were

mounted in the fort and the Confederate was able to muster ninety-nine. This might allow you sir, and the gentlemen, to gauge the intensity of noise which seemed to go unlimited, hour after hour. The like of it I have never experienced before and please God, will not do so again. At one point I truly felt day had visited night.

Now I must relate a strange set of events that were put into motion around midday of the 13th. The incident started with the flag-pole at the fort being struck. Those on the land assumed the fort had capitulated. While this was being enacted a certain Senator, Mr Louis Wigfall, had rowed out to the fort, unbeknown to one and all. It transpired that the gentleman in question did secure an agreement and the occupants of the fort were prepared to withdraw. However, when Major Anderson discovered the Senator had no authority, it took a while for the Confederate's aides, who had then arrived, to calm the major. The upshot was that the next day, the 14th at 2 p.m., the cannon salute began at the fort in honour of the Union flag.

The garrison then started to withdraw by small boats to the Union ships waiting at anchor near the mouth of the bay. Soon after the evacuation had been completed by the Union force, shortly after 4 p.m, General P. G. T. Beauregard took possession of the fort. Charleston abounded with jubilant celebrations. What was truly a miracle was that, in the thirty-three hours of conflict during which 3,341 projectiles were fired at the fort, no Union soldier was wounded or killed, although four were grazed by portions of brick shrapnel. Paradoxically, during the salute two men were killed in an accident and four injured in the consequential explosion. For the Confederates, four men sustained injuries. Thus was the toll of this conflict.

Sir, I beg your indulgence if I stop writing at this time; I am overcome by emotions and exhaustion. With your approval I will send this letter without delay and complete my report on the situation in the next few days.

Sir, you will appreciate that at present matters of the future are unresolved. The company's destiny cannot be determined until I have assembled the facts.

It feels strange that these tragic events should have been enacted on the Sabbath; how mortal and frail is man.

I am, and remain, your obedient servant. . .

Three
Patriotism

Richmond
21 April 1861

Sir,

Having gathered all information of use in Charleston, I considered additional information might best be obtained here in Richmond. During my stay I have made useful contacts in both the civilian and military establishments. These good people do not feel the need for restraint in my presence; all are keen to seek friendly relationships with Her Majesty's government, thus I am able to conclude my unfinished correspondence.

Again, for sake of clarity, I shall relate the information in chronological sequence.

As stated in my previous correspondence, when the states seceded there were problems regarding government establishments and property, especially those of the military. Swift action secured most of them for the Confederacy. There were a number of fortifications within the Confederacy that were occupied in strength by the Union. They were reinforced soon after President Lincoln's speech. That part referring to property is now clear as to intent.

The President considered Forts Picken and Taylor, on the Florida southern coast, were of great importance should war come. Then there was Fort Sumpter, and the other forts in the mouth of Charleston harbour. Fort Monroe, located on the coast of Virginia, was another whose position was especially important as it could be the landing stage for an advance on Richmond. The two Florida forts were speedily reinforced. However, attempts to supply the forts of Charleston were thwarted from the outset.

South Carolina was well aware of the danger should these forts remain occupied by the Union. Thus began a confused state of affairs. When the Union tried to reinforce the forts, this was claimed to be an act of aggression by the Confederates, whereas the Union claimed the Confederacy to be threatening the forts.

The south considered it an aggressive move when the Union commander moved all units into Fort Sumpter, by far the strongest and best located to control all shipping into the harbour. The north claimed the move was simply an act of defence. When various ships were sent by the Union, the Confederates took counter-measures to prevent the ships reaching their destination. I have learned that the fort was poorly stocked with food and munitions. Without extra supplies there was little hope of survival.

Warships and troops were sent, but arrived a day too late. Thus they could only return whence they came with the garrison from the fort. The South Carolinans were resolute, whereas the Union seemed indecisive on this matter. Now the newspapers have joined battle, each exalting patriotism, the South calling people to arms to defend the Confederacy, the North intent on punishing the errant states for the Fort Sumpter insult. Here in Richmond, the attitude and mood was expressed by one article.

'The guns have spoken. Like a sword when it cut the Gordian knot, the cannon has sliced through a tangle of issue that men failed to resolve for over half a century. North and South no longer have to confront slavery, state rights, or reconciliation. There is now the chance to resolve all, once and for all, in the time-honoured manner, by force of arms.'

President Lincoln was appealing to all countrymen to seek out the better angels of their nature: all must remain friends. The general attitude of the northern populace was that the angels could no longer help, for Confederates and Unionists were now mortal enemies.

There is confusion in my mind. No clear directive has emanated from Washington or Richmond that a conflict has indeed started. I have quizzed travellers from Washington as to the views held by the populace there. They confirm them to be similar to those abounding in Richmond. All are relieved that the arguments and debates are now concluded, and everyone is sure of victory in any outcome of arms. In the meantime, most newspapers have unleashed an uncompromising barrage of words, helping to fan the flames of war.

The other confusion in my mind relates to the military. I fell into conversation with certain officers resident in Richmond. Their whole manner was very matter of fact, displaying extreme casualness towards the prospect of war as if it were a natural event. Many mentioned fellow officers with whom they had been friends in the military training academy and who now professed loyalty to the Union. What struck me as strangest of all was that these friends, now likely to be on opposing sides, bade each other farewell and good fortune, declaring the war would not cause a rift in their friendship.

The academy I referred to above is an establishment which receives young gentlemen from all over the land to train in the art of good officership. Have we the like in the United Kingdom?

What is most incomprehensible of all is the outcome should there be a battle. Wars to date have been fought between differing nationalities; this war will not conform to that idea.

England is host to small numbers of people from other countries, and the number of their countries of origin is also small. That is not the case here; both peoples and countries represented greatly outnumber those in the United Kingdom, my guess is by at least three times or more. Indeed, should the armies take to the field they will each be cosmopolitan in compilation. I can foresee Greek against Greek, German against German, Irish against Irish, English against English, and so on. The difference compared to Europe, so far as I am able to discern, lies in the fact that in Europe a nation is constrained within its boundaries. However, in this country the people do not have such a constraint, and thus are in communities scattered across the length and breadth of this land. Most surprising of all, their cultural loyalty will not be their binding factor, but where they dwell will be paramount, and so their loyalty will be to the state.

The recruitment of any army has taken a step backwards in one respect. It is not unlike the situation in medieval times when Barons and Lords each recruited men. Now it is the states who fill this role and will be in command of such regiments. From this situation it will be the decision of each state as to the extent of their contribution. I understand both Washington and Richmond have sent out proclamations to each state and territory, setting figures for recruitment.

Both sides are seeking men to join for six months' duration. The tone is that they are needed for defence. The military are boasting that any conflict will be over in six months, and see no reason to ask those who enlist to be away from their homes for a longer period.

This state of peace and war is puzzling in the extreme. The uncertainty leaves me no other recourse than to proceed with caution regarding the company's enterprise. Sir, I do have your concurrence, and that of the honourable Board, to my proposal? Should this matter be resolved in the six months as predicted, I see it as causing minimal delay to my work.

Before I next write, I feel it desirable to visit Washington to ascertain the future policy of the Union administration. This is important as I am of the firm opinion that, should there be an act of aggression, the Union has the stronger causes for acting. My reasoning is based on the fact that the Union has a population numbering around twenty million, compared to only nine million in the Confederacy. Furthermore the north greatly outstrips the south in almost every department and resource.

I trust, sir, that you and the gentlemen of the Board have confidence in me to continue the company's enterprise even in the face of temporary adversity.

I am, and remain, your obedient servant. . .

Washington
30 April 1861

Sir,

I arrived a few days ago following a tolerable journey. There is a bridge that traverses the River Potomac from the Virginian side and leads directly to Washington. The fellow guarding the bridge seemed affable and courteous, paying only the minimum attention to travellers. This did not indicate a state of war to me, or even a readiness for it. If the imminence of the war were truly felt then I would have expected greater alertness on the part of the guards: vigilance would have been essential, as enemy soil supported one end of the bridge while their own capital was but a stone's throw away at the other end. Viewing Washington from the Potomac under the present situation made me realize that here is a relatively new-born capital, merely sixty years old, which has grown to 63,000 inhabitants. This place of a few government buildings and a cluster of mansions will be where war is directed. For the rest it is a shanty town, and beyond that open fields. Surely war could not be conducted thus?

When I finally entered the place, I quickly espied the signs of war: soldiers encamped in every available space, marching and drilling in arms. This was not a trained army by any means. There was a general concern that the place could expect an attack at any moment, due to its close proximity to the enemy.

It might be of importance, whilst on the subject of preparedness, to mention that one-fifth of the people of the Union are from Ireland, Germany, and Great Britain, with lesser numbers from Poland, Scandinavia, Holland and Italy. Throughout the Union only one per cent are of African origins. Sadly, most in the north and the south consider the negroes, be they free or in slavery, as a race apart. I learned that some fifteen million of the people dwell and work on the land and in small towns, the latter comparable in size to large English villages.

News came to me that on 19th April in the town of Baltimore in Maryland state, there was a serious confrontation between the Sixth Massachusetts regiment and an organized group of secessionists, resulting in the deaths of three soldiers and twenty civilians. Further, twenty soldiers were injured and one hundred and thirty reported missing. Soon after this bloodshed, the secessionists in Baltimore destroyed bridges and other communications to prevent the passage of troops to defend Washington.

General Butler however, found an alternative overland route that did not touch upon Baltimore. He and the Eighth Massachusetts, along with the Seventh New York regiment, arrived in Washington on 25th April.

The capital has been in a state of alarm since Virginia seceded on 17th April. There were rumours that thirty thousand Confederate troops were massing in northern Virginia. Four days ago, Governor Hicks called the Maryland legislature into session at Frederick, located fifty miles to the west of Baltimore and eighteen miles from Harper's Ferry. There was rumour that Maryland intended to secede. This would place Washington in a difficult position, the more so since a delegation from Baltimore had visited the President to ask that no federal troops should pass through the state of Maryland. The delegation's mission failed.

Would there now have to be a battle for Maryland? In the military, lines were being drawn. Most officers declared their loyalty for their home state, thus many left the Union army. The matter now became critical for President Lincoln since Virginia had taken the fatal decision. The seventy-five year old General-in-Chief Winfield Scott and a Colonel Robert E. Lee, also a General Joseph E. Johnston, were all Virginians.

I have been told the General-in-Chief declined to resign: his loyalty was to the Union. General Johnston elected to resign. What came as a surprise was the case of Colonel Lee, the Harper's Ferry victor. Would he take command of the Union army? On the 18th he declined. He considered secession wrong, and disliked slavery, yet was unable to up the sword against his state. He could not draw his sword for any cause, save in defence of Virginia.

Strangely, other officers from the south elected to serve the Union. In all, 313 officers did resign, depleting the officership of the Union by one third: a severe blow for the President. The Union navy lost 373 out of 1,554 officers.

Indeed, this end of April is a time of possible adversity in the capital. The initial euphoria is on the wane. The scourge which can so easily eat away at confidence is doubt. If the capital is in imminent danger of capture, what hope is there for the Union?

On that sombre note I conclude this letter and shall write further as events proceed. My intention is to stay a short while longer, then return to Richmond.

I am, and remain, your obedient servant. . .

Richmond
20 May 1861

Sir,

This day I learned news that has heartened the Confederacy, and which I assume will add to the Union's problems.

Initially on 1st May, Tennessee voted to support the Confederacy, which step may have prompted others to act. Thus, Arkansas seceded on 6th May and today the state of North Carolina seceded. All about me I see faces full of pleasure.

The latest news restored confidence. Recently news has been received that Union troops occupied important positions near Baltimore on 5th May, and on 13th May did in fact occupy Baltimore itself. The officer responsible for this was the commander of the Sixteenth Massachusetts regiment. It would appear Washington had taken a decision regarding Maryland, and there seemed little likelihood that Maryland would now be free to decide whether to secede or not. The grip was further tightened with arrests of prominent personages who were outspoken against war and classed as secessionists. My opinion is that Maryland will be a thorn in the side of the Union president.

Reviewing the situation, I feel it is now possible to apply vigorous efforts with regards to the company's enterprise here in the Confederacy. I would also urge you, sir, and the gentlemen of the Board, to expedite the New York matter: the moment is right. With an army that needs to be trained and its command in disarray I cannot visualize a threat from the Union for at least two years. The Union government is indecisive, with little likelihood of firm policies until 1862. There also exists internal unrest, and there are other pressing national matters. I am also sure the secessionists and southern sympathizers will be mischievous, provoke demonstrations and generally create diversions and mayhem in many forms. Thus I expect the Union government will have much to occupy its attention for the best part of 1862 and even 1863. By the time these matters are resolved the Confederacy will have been established in the international sphere, in addition to its own internal development that would then allow it to stand on equal terms with the Union.

This is now the time to explore in depth the route I previously undertook, through the states of the Confederacy. My objective will be to seek locations in which to set up offices from whence to operate our enterprise.

Thereafter I envisage having to spend time in each location in order to determine the objectives of trade for each office. In this vast land, needs and requirements will differ greatly according to population and terrain. Unless I receive instructions to the contrary I shall proceed with my preparations and planning. It should take a month before I am able to set forth. There should be little difficulty in communicating to you from the various stops en route.

I am, and remain, your obedient servant. . .

Richmond
26 June 1861

Sir,

My preparations are almost concluded and I should commence my expedition by the end of the month.

There have been developments since last I wrote. Tennessee finally seceded on 8th June. General Lee is military advisor to President Davis and General Joseph E. Johnston, the Commander-in-Chief of the Confederate army, a most formidable and admired general. The Confederacy star has indeed truly began its ascent.

Before departing I must inform you of some minor news, though this should in no way deter or delay my forthcoming mission. Newly promoted Major General Butler took command of Fort Monroe on 22nd May. This may prove a minor irritation to Richmond.

Not unexpectedly, yet a little out of character, the Union responded to Virginia's secession. The following day, under the command of Brigadier General Irvin McDowell, eleven regiments seized a small area of land on the south side of the Potomac, across from Washington. The reason for this move was simply to safeguard their capital.

The attack apparently commenced at the unearthly hour of 2 a.m. To the right three regiments crossed and occupied Arlington, including the home of General Lee. They moved forward and cut the railway linking Alexandria with Leesburg. At the same time, another regiment occupied Arlington Heights, while yet a third regiment advanced and captured Alexandria after a brief exchange of fire. The Confederates were forced to withdraw.

During the day's action the Union lost a popular officer. InnkeeperJames Jackson became a hero of the south when he shot and killed the Union Colonel Ellsworthy in Alexandra's marshall-house. The Colonel had foolishly climbed to the roof to cut down the flag and, whilst descending, was shot by Jackson who in turn was struck down by one Corporal Brownell. For some strange reason, unfathomable to me, the North went into mourning for this officer, and momentarily it seemed to have infused enthusiasm into the flagging spirits of the Union.

Confederate troops are now stationed in Yorktown and Big Bethel to observe Union activities in Fort Monroe. Colonel Magruder commands the force in Yorktown and the Peninsula, and has dispatched Colonel Hill to Big Bethel where he has constructed earthworks after the fashion of those used in the Crimea, but more restricted because of the marshes and woodland.

The conflict involved some 1,400 Confederates and 4,400 Unionists, and commenced around 8 a.m. Prior to that, two Union regiments fired upon one another by mistake; twenty-one soldiers died or were wounded.

From details explained to me by an officer, the Union troops were surprise by the earthworks and ill prepared to attack. Each side exchanged cannon fire to little effect, the Union assault lasting barely two hours before they withdrew in disarray to Fort Monroe. The cost to the Confederates was one man dead and ten wounded, while the Union suffered eighteen dead and fifty wounded.

General Butler had the First, Second, Third and Fifth New York regiments plus the First Vermont and his own Fourth Massachusetts. The Confederate regiments were the First North Carolinas and Third Virginians. This demonstrates the composition of likely armies and supports my comments in previous letters.

One other event of minor importance occurred in West Virginia when people were seeking to break from the rest of Virginia and join the Union. To counter this, President Lincoln sent a small force to seize the railway that connects Harper's Ferry to the Ohio River, a route vital for supplies and troops from the west. Meanwhile, Colonel Kelly set out from Wheeling and Brigadier General Morris set out from Pakersburgh, their aim being to capture the Confederate force of 733 men at Grafton.

Colonel Porterfield was aware of the situation and withdrew to the village of Philippi, south of Grafton, where the enemy surprised him on 3rd June, but he was able to withdraw, thus saving his force but leaving the 3,000-strong Union force in control. I understand the man who planned the invasion was Major General McClellan of the Ohio Command.

My impression is that both events were small-scale and of no real importance: The Confederacy has lost nothing, the Union has gained little. Their two incursions might represent a threat had there been any real intent, but the size of their forces contradicts the idea of an invasion.

What is of amazement to me are the recent newspaper articles reporting General Scott's plan to the President, which plan was to starve the Confederacy by capturing all installations and fortifications along the Mississippi River. Attempts to blockade along the coast would be both difficult and costly, and would indeed be a siege on a grandiose scale, never as yet attempted in history. Lay siege to a nation. The mind shudders; thus I am confident the Union will realize that the mammoth task of attempting to subdue the Confederacy is out of the question. All concerned here say the action by the Union is purely defensive, therefore I have no qualms about departing on my journey.

I am, and remain, your obedient servant. . .

Richmond
26 June 1861

My dearest mother,

Please forgive your son for not writing to you sooner. I have been lost in time in this giant land.

Yes, mother, it is the only word that can adequately express this land of America with its towering mountains, wide rivers, huge areas of woodlands, and fields that reach to the horizon. It is difficult to describe the variety of landscapes encountered, and how quickly you can plunged from one type to another. One moment you look on a barren panorama, and around the next bend there is luscious vegetation. Towns are great distances from each other, and it can take more than a day to travel from one to the next. Many places named on the map comprise no more than a dozen timber-built dwellings. The roads are nothing more than dirt tracks, although many are well used. These are usually given the name of turnpikes. The majority of the people seem to stay near to their homes, but a few do roam. Travel for these, when they do venture away, is usually by horseback. Once I encountered a prairie schooner, which is an enormous wagon with a fabric that can be used to form a roof to cover it. The contraption is drawn by six horses, and can accommodate the entire contents of a house. It can also support and nourish a family on their trek of a hundred miles or longer.

New York I liken to London: in many ways it is similar, but it has a more cosmopolitan population than London. This I suppose is due to the port being the place where all arriving in this country first disembark. They stay close by for a year or longer, until the urge comes to move on and seek their fortune in the land beyond.

London I found to have a number of religions, all under the one banner of Christianity. New York has a greater variety of religions, with services conducted in many tongues. The services in the churches, chapels, or wherever people can meet, tend to be extremely noisy, and the congregations openly and unashamedly express their emotion with gestures and chants. It is a strange experience when first encountered, but it can also embrace you in the atmosphere in a short time.

Little did I know what lay ahead of me when Uncle Silas selected me to come here. The customs are so different from those in England especially how they form their government. The land is divided into states, and each governs itself, yet at the same time the states elect members to form a national governing body in Washington. Beyond that I have no information on the subject.

Similar to the United Kingdom, this country also has two main political groups, yet within these two groups many differing views are held. For example on the matter of slavery, there are factions in both parties in favour of slavery whilst others oppose slavery. It is all too puzzling for me at present.

I must now stop and post this to you. Time will elapse before I can write again because I am about to travel on the rail network of this immense land for Uncle Silas and the company

I am, and remain, your loving son. . .

Four
Is this really war?

Bristol, Tennessee
5 July 1861

Sir,

I arrived here soon after noon and hope to spend several days surveying the area. It has the advantage of being close to the borders of Virginia and North Carolina. The previous place of Lynchburg was close to Richmond and therefore would not have been of use.

Firstly, Bristol is ideally situated to serve various townships radiating from here, by means of the prairie schooners. From my conversations with the Mayor I understand the terrain, as well as being mountainous in parts, has many rivers and tributaries but lacks household goods and implements, cloth and ironmongery, there being a serious shortage of iron and steel. The people manage to scrape a livelihood but struggle against the land and the weather, so their financial state is poor at present. In the long term, as the Confederacy prospers, so a portion of that wealth will filter to these people, thus increasing trade.

My conclusion is to apply caution in the short term: to establish an office in 1862 or 1863 and develop from a small beginning. I would rate this project as a second, or perhaps third priority.

It is my intention to stay a further two days to talk with others to confirm the information given me by the Mayor. The good fellow has the concern of Bristol at heart and earnestly wishes it to prosper and grow, but he fears that the community may fade into a ghost town. He claims many such do exist, where people have given up the fight. My impression of the townsfolk, however, is that they are as yet untouched by all the events happening in the east; life may be described as hard, challenging, yet they possess a determined satisfaction. This is not a place for the faint-hearted; it is for the tough, optimistic breed.

Through the telegraphic system I received the following: Major General McClellan has been reinforcing his Union army in West Virginia. It now numbers 20,000 and appear to be deployed around Grafton. The Confederates have a new commander, Brigadier General Garnett, who has assembled a force of 6,000 near Beverly. The Union policy appears to be one of protecting West Virginia and the newly elected Governor Mr Pierpont, whereas the Confederate force has taken up a purely defensive position on Laurel and Rich Mountains.

Unfortunately the Union army seems intent on a confrontation. They marched to within ten miles of the Confederate force by 2nd July. I fear the Confederates are in a hostile area of Virginia and need to be vigilant.

I have delayed this letter due to the conflict on 11th July, yesterday. Brigadier General Rosecrans attacked and finally captured Rich Mountain where the vastly outnumbered Confederates put up a spirited fight before having to give ground. Mistakenly the Union commander had considered Rich Mountain to be where the main enemy force was concentrated. This prove unfortunate for the gallant Confederates.

Today is 13th July and brings sad news. The force of 555 were not able to join their comrades on Mount Laurel and so surrendered to the Union army. Brigadier General Garnett did yesterday withdraw from the mountain in order to conserve his force until the advantage of ground was his.

Sir, I did warn that matters have a habit of happening with great rapidity in this land. There has been an exchange of fire at Garrick's Ford, during which Brigadier General Garnett was struck dead. The main force of Confederates are now safely out of reach of the enemy.

There is a report that on 3rd June a Colonel Porterfield did skilfully withdraw his entire force and supplies from Philippi when the Unionist Colonel Kelly and his force opened fired with cannon at dawn. They had marched through atrocious weather the previous day and night to achieve the surprise.

This clash does mean that West Virginia will probably join the Union in the future. It might also mean that the State of Kentucky could be restrained from joining the Confederacy; a minor set-back, but one that should not delay the Confederacy's increased prosperity.

I have delayed departure due to events. Now I will leave tomorrow for that strange-sounding place, Chattanooga, from where I shall next write.

I am, and remain, your obedient servant. . .

Chattanooga, Tennessee
16 July 1861

Sir,

I arrived yesterday evening and was glad to refresh the inner and outer man. This morning I did search out the mayor, a forthright fellow, similar to his counterpart in Bristol. He presides over the township like a parent.

The River Tennessee traverses a great portion of southern Tennessee eastwards, then widens westwards in the direction of the Mississippi River. It is navigable even allowing for its many bends en route.

This place is a junction of three rail links: one east to Richmond, one west to the River Mississippi, and one south through the state of Georgia. The south approach abounds with creeks whereas few are to be found to the north. There is a group of towns to the south within a distance of some twenty to thirty miles. To the north of the river are a few small settlements.

The mountain terrain is still in evidence and Chattanooga looks picturesque in the valley with the twisting river. The sides of the mountains have large boulders, many grotesque in appearance. It made me feel as if I were looking upon a stone-age scene. In a word, I would sum up the whole area as rugged; the same can be said of the people who dwell here.

Because of the creeks there is a reasonable water source, thus agriculture thrives, but not on a grand scale. Timber is also available. Chattanooga is close to the northern borders of Georgia and Alabama which may have future prospects. Thus, subject to further investigations, I consider it will be possible to list this a 'priority two' project for 1862. It will be no problem to construct an office and living accommodation from natural resources.

Today, 18th July, I fell into conversation with a learned gentleman who did enlighten me further of the situation regarding the states of Kentucky and Missouri. My previous correspondence on the matter was woefully incomplete, and so I feel I should acquaint you, sir, and the Board, as to the importance of this additional information.

The rivers greatly supplement the few railways in the Confederacy. Rivers in the east tend to flow west to east and are only navigable for short lengths, useful as defence barriers. The rivers of the west by contrast, are bigger and fully navigable, but more importantly, flow north to south. It is along some of these rivers that a useful implement of war can be used, namely, the gunboat. I mention the expected value of these rivers for war purposes as this also demonstrates their use commercially.

The Mississippi flows between St Louis and Memphis, a distance of 250 miles, where it is joined by the Ohio and the Missouri. The Ohio is important for movement of men and supplies from the industrial east to any western theatre of war. One of its tributaries flows into Alabama, useful for an invading force; the other, the Cumberland, leads to the major industrial centre of Nashville. The Missouri serves the states further west.

These two states, with their large populations, would be a prize to either the Union or the Confederacy. Their combined sources could boost the Confederacy by 25 per cent.

With Kentucky in the Union there is a chance that Tennessee may be lost to the Confederacy. However if the reverse should happen, then the threat to the Union could be serious with the loss of the Ohio foundries and mills. It would also threaten the coal and iron-ore traffic.

It is held that should Missouri secede, then Kentucky will follow, thus blocking Kansas and south Illinois. However, should both join the south, which will greatly boost the increase of prosperity in which the company would share, I fear this would, out of necessity, provoke military action by the Union, which to date has not shown signs of serious intent.

Richmond and Washington are extremely sensitive in their dealings with the two states; the decision is balanced by a hair's breadth. Both are seeking aid. However, as power is so finely balanced within these states it is impossible for them to aid or succour any neighbour.

President Lincoln's taking office was a signal for raiders from Kansas, nicknamed 'jayhawkers', to increase their activities in Missouri. Naturally there were reprisals by a gang with the nickname of 'border ruffians'.

My learned friend has been able to acquaint me with the latest information from Missouri, as follows. A Republican Congressman is leading an effort against Governor Jackson, a pro-southerner. This gentleman manipulated the return to Washington of the senior officer, thus allowing his ally, a Captain Lyon, to take command. The Captain safeguarded an arsenal then took prisoners, a group of pro-southern militia. On 10th May he paraded them through the streets of St Louis, thus provoking a riot. By the end of the day one soldier was dead and one wounded. Twenty-eight civilians were killed, two of whom were women, also a baby; a further sixty-two were injured. A bloody day indeed.

By 12th May, 3,000 pro-southerners had fled and St Louis

was firmly in Union hands. The scales no longer were balanced. Both sides prepared for battle, General Price and Governor Jackson for the Confederates, opposed by Congressman Blair, and the now-promoted Brigadier General Lyons.

On 10th June the Union occupied the capital, Jefferson City. Shortly after there was a skirmish at Boonsville which was short in duration. The strength of both sides was around 6,000.

The new Union commander is Major General Fremont; his opponent, Major General Polk.

At Carthage, Colonel Sigel of the Union force did battle with Governor Jackson's force on 5th July. The Union side broke off the engagement. Dead were thirteen Unionists and ten Confederates. So the contest rages as to whose arms will prevail to take the spoils of Missouri.

Sir, I intend to stay one more day and plan to depart the day after. In the meantime I shall observe with keen interest the outcome of the struggle for Missouri. If all goes well and the Confederates win the day, then this should bode well for the company.

I am, and remain, your obedient servant. . .

Memphis, Tennessee
22 July 1861

Sir,

I am now arrived at this bustling port which is a veritable hive of industry involving many vessels.

Tomorrow I intend to observe the activities of the port with respect to its function, regulations and types of trade.

I am now writing on this day, 24th July, having completed my first task. There are various goods being landed ready for distribution inland. As yet I have been unable to determine if there are any commodities lacking or not supplied.

This day, 25th July, I had a walk around the place. It is sprawling in design, with imposing buildings along the east bank, the less elegant houses behind. Beyond these, on the perimeter of the town, are numerous constructions of timber and of a basic, austere design where many people of African origin dwell. Rising in the distance is a magnificent range of hills, standing as if a natural screen for the town below.

My conclusion is that this town will grow, expand its trade and prosper in time. I therefore rate it as a priority three, for consideration in 1864.

News is reaching here of further conflicts, although my impression is that these have not yet taken on the guise of war: they are more a question of manoeuvring to create buffers as a means of protection and defence. The forces engaged to date have been relatively small.

The Confederacy has fortified Harper's Ferry, which changed hands during June without bloodshed, and is massing 10,000 men under General Johnston, in the lush lands of Shenandoah, Virginia.

In the meantime, I understand Union General McDowell has amassed a staggering 35,000 troops. George Washington's entire Yorktown army was a mere 16,000. Opposing him will be General Beauregard, with a force of almost equal size. Surely this is not to be the ultimate battle?

The Confederates were in a good position to defend along the Bull Run River between Centreville and Manassas Junction.

General McDowell's army moved on 16th July.

On 18th July a Union force was repulsed at the southern end of the Confederate line. On the northern end of the line a Union force had crossed a ford on the Bull Run River, and was advancing on the weakest part of the Confederate six-mile line of defence. The outnumbered Confederates were able to delay the Union troops for several hours, thus allowing reinforcements to arrive at the battleground of Matthews Hill. There had been a number of bayonet charges by both sides. Temporarily, the Union troops had distracted the Confederates a little to the south, which delayed the reinforcements being sent to Matthews Hill. Sadly after two hours, some Union troops moved north into the rear of Matthews Hill, thus the Confederates had no option but to retreat. The Union troops reformed before pursuit, as their attacks back at the hill had been piecemeal. The battle was about to be renewed at Young's Branch, then shift to Henry House Hill.

I understand that at this time many Confederate reinforcements were arriving from Shenandoah to help bolster the line. The turning point came around 2 p.m. when Union guns were seized. These were to change hands several times over the next two hours with considerable losses on both sides.

Around 4 p.m. fresh Confederate troops from the railway at Manassas Junction did rout a Union Brigade. The Confederates seized the advantage and their whole line advanced. Union troops started a disorganized retreat around 4.30 p.m. and were pursued; however the plan to cut off their retreat at Centreville did not succeed and at seven o'clock the battle ended, the large

Union army defeated by the determination of the Confederate soldiers. I did hear that civilians came out of Washington to watch the battle, the like of which I have never heard before.

Both armies blundered and misjudgements were made. This confirmed my previous opinion that the troops of the Union need much training, more so than those of the Confederacy who seemed consumed by fire and fervour with the added incentive of defending their land and liberty. I am still of the opinion that, although many of the inexperienced Union soldiers did exhibit bravery, it will take two years to construct a fully trained army, made the more difficult by short-term service. By then the Confederation will be strong.

There were apparently moments of confusion that contributed to fateful consequences, when enemy troops encountered each other and were not recognized as friend or foe until the last moment; there were several occasions when troops fired on their own. Initial figures indicate 2,000 casualties which includes 387 dead, while Union losses were put at around 3,000 of which 470 were dead. There are many recriminations in Washington which will surely delay any further action until long and deliberate debate has been concluded.

My view is that the Union will content itself with the ground it commands and rest its main army around Washington and along the north bank of the River Potomac, both of these being defensive in nature and design. It is stalemate and thus I feel the survey and plans for the company may now proceed unhindered. With my business here concluded I shall take a train tomorrow for the town known as Jackson, the first stop on the southern section of my tour.

Sir, I am, and remain, your obedient servant. . .

Jackson, Mississippi
28 July 1861

Sir,

This day I did arrive in the late afternoon. The line between Memphis and Jackson was bedevilled with problems that drastically extended the journey time.

Once accommodation had been found, duly refreshed I did investigate in greater depth the matter of railways.

Jackson had three railway companies with tracks into the town, but only the Southern Mississippi track actually passes through. This starts in the obscurity of Alabama, passes through

Selma to the east, and terminates in the large, well-populated centre of Vicksburg on the Mississippi River, to the west. I have marked Vicksburg for investigation at a later date. The Mississippi Central from Memphis terminates to the north of Jackson. The New Orleans, Jackson, and Great Northern railway commences from the south side of the town and will be part of my route south.

Sir, you and the members of the Board will readily be aware of the problem regarding transference of goods between the three companies: all goods would have to be manhandled and hauled betwixt each. This is typical of many junctions throughout the Confederacy; no small wonder when for the 9,000 miles of track there are 113 owners. The major causes for the transfer system are the many different sizes of gauge adopted.

As to Jackson itself; it is the capital of the State of Mississippi and is spacious in layout with trees used to good effect. Although I have written of Jackson as being a capital my first impression remains, that it is more akin to a town than a city. Touring the place I did discover it to be a manufacturing source, whereas I have in the main encountered trading centres throughout my journey to date. There are foundries, machine-shops, warehouses, factories, arsenals and public stores. I see no reason why these should not be exploited. It has ready-made facilities, and no doubt the owners would be keen to serve our requirements. The town is ideal in location with potentially large markets, possibly in Montgomery, but certainly in New Orleans, Vicksburg and Memphis where raw materials could be landed. I feel sure the railway problem can be resolved if the companies come to appreciate the gain in increased profits.

I have been fortunate to have secured a room at the hotel, which I understand is the only one in the capital. There is a need, therefore, for a second hotel in the immediate future, with others later as expansion develops. I do strongly urge you to despatch an appointed representative to pursue the matter as a first priority. In view of Jackson's potential, I shall delay departure for a few days to explore the surrounding area to the east and to make a brief visit to Vicksburg.

I am returned from my foray today, 2nd August, and it has been extremely pleasant; the terrain is pleasing to the eye. There are many communities to the east served by dirt tracks. Vicksburg is unlike any other town I have thus far visited; it has the appearance and atmosphere of orderliness plus several distinctive features, visible for miles. My previous conviction has been greatly reinforced as the result of my trip: I do perceive Jackson to be the basin out of which, in time, vast communities will be served.

Tomorrow I shall spend as a day of rest, and propose to set forth for New Orleans on the following day. I have not been able to ascertain any war reports. These people seemed unconcerned with matters in the east; many view it as political bickering which avails them nothing. As is human nature there are a few who do debate feebly the pros and cons of Unionism and Confederacy, but most agree it is far away from them, and their trade and businesses are flourishing sufficiently for them to have no foreboding as to the future.

Sir, I am, and remain, your obedient servant. . .

New Orleans, Louisiana
6 August 1861

Sir,

The journey did pass through varied and interesting terrain, in parts similar to the rural scenes of England.

New Orleans is betwixt a northern inland lake, with access to the Gulf of Mexico and, to the south, the Mississippi River whose estuary is the Gulf of Mexico. Over the years, many people from different parts of the world have settled here which is what gives the place its colour.

French influence in architecture, customs and language dominates the area. In particular I am interested in the Creole people who appear to be native to the area, and many of whom are handsome and beauteous in feature with a quaint French speech. The inhabitants live a vigorous existence and there are numerous recognized established families. The community as a whole is ambitious for wealth by whatever means, and newcomers need to be on the alert for rogues and swindlers. I have been told the duel is still the means whereby disputes are settled and that rivalry and feuding are rife, but I have seen no evidence of this. Perhaps these things are conducted discreetly, in the same fashion as the French amour. It is claimed this place is second only to Richmond in manufacturing, which explains the apparent wealth.

These impressions I have placed on record to present you, sir, and the honourable gentlemen of the Board with the likely atmosphere and conditions, should it be decided to trade with New Orleans. The port is extremely busy, being the only one of consequence along the entire southern coastline of the Confederacy. I would recommend the port facilities be used to import goods and material destined for the west of the Mississippi River, whence they would need to be transported by wagon, as I understand rivers and railroads are almost nonexistent. Certain materials may be suitable for carriage by rail to Jackson; however, for the bulk of goods and materials the River Mississippi to Vicksburg will prove the safer, quicker and more efficient route.

Conversing with certain citizens I have come to the conclusion they are, one and all, oblivious of matters in the east.

I do intend to stay but a short time in this place, only long enough to verify the above information as correct. Part of that time will be spent seeking passage by ship to the town of Mobile, further east along the coast. From there I will be able to entrain for the eastward part of my journey.

My next communication will be sent from Mobile.

Sir, I am, and remain, your obedient servant. . .

New Orleans, Louisiana
7 August 1861

My dearest mother,

It does not seem possible that I landed in America in mid-September last year, and have since spent most of my time travelling.

I do miss the tranquillity of East Anglia and the estate. Nature was gentle compared to the aggressiveness of things out here. When people describe the land as wild and untamed I know what they mean.

On my travels I did find a peace and sanctuary in a few of the communities, but most are bustling with activities, as each person seeks to improve his lot in life. No one is ashamed to make a fortune because there are plenty of opportunities to do so. This is a young nation compared to those established in Europe, Africa and Asia.

On the subject of nations you have no doubt heard of the conflict here, and how a number of states have broken away from the Union of States to form their own group known as the Confederacy. Sadly it seems the hotheads have prevailed and there might be war to resolve the dispute. To date small numbers of armed men have fought in various parts of the continent, but all the skirmishes were brief, and on such a small scale that I do not think I can, in all honesty, call them battles. But as in any conflict large or small, people die or are terribly wounded. If this conflict is to escalate into a proper war then many thousands of families will be touched by grief.

Those directly involved are in the area of Richmond and Washington, whilst the rest of the scattered and remote populace seemed unaffected, and life goes on normally.

I did mention travel, which is an extraordinary experience. The carriages are austere, with wooden seats, and ventilation is by means of windows, but there is a choice, to ventilate and suffer the dust or perspire profusely. It can take days to travel between destinations. I was told there are nine thousand miles of rail track throughout America owned by one hundred and thirteen companies. Nothing is uniform between these companies, which causes innumerable problems; some of the tracks end in wildernesses because it was not profitable to continue to the nearest community before terminating.

Time now dictates that I leave off writing, so I will write you again, dear mother, at the earliest possible opportunity.

Your loving son. . .

Five
Home to Richmond

Mobile, Alabama
13 August 1861

Sir,

The journey by ship I had calculated to be no more than two days from New Orleans; however this was not so. The ship did set sail around midday on the tenth. Then the master did anchor in the estuary until dusk. When I questioned the meaning of this action, the master informed me that it was necessary to ensure no interception by one of a number of Union warships which was attempting a blockade. This was indeed a shock.

Further delay was encountered when by dawn we arrived at the entrance to Mobile Bay. There we had to anchor while the Confederate navy investigated all in a most thorough manner. Yet another delay occurred whilst an opening was made through the obstacles across the entrance. The master drew my attention to the three forts we passed before arriving at Mobile: the forts of Morgan, Gaines and Powell, appearing formidable in construction. Two other items of information were presented to me: only seafarers with knowledge of the channels can navigate the area owing to the many shoals; the other disturbing item was related to Fort Pickens, some miles eastward along the coast that stands at the entrance to the small port of Pensacola. This is the only one of the many forts along the entire southern coastline still garrisoned by Union forces. Indeed at the time of the Fort Sumpter incident, Fort Pickens was the only fort not to be occupied by the Confederates. The Union did in fact reinforce the bastion.

The master reassured me there were few problems with the blockading warships: the Union does not have sufficient ships for the task and therefore it is simple for ships to run the blockade. The reassurance did not fill me with confidence. The moment I set foot on land I immediately purchased a ticket for the first available train departing from Mobile.

It will be necessary for me to reappraise the risk factors involved in using the port of New Orleans. One possibility is that the blockade will cease within the next year, when the Confederacy is established as a member of the world community. However I do rule out the port of Mobile being suitable for the company's requirements. I can find no adverse reason why the Jackson recommendation should be cancelled. Sir, I will immediately inform you and the Board should the situation change.

My next report will be from Montgomery where I hope to learn details of the current situation with regards to the confrontation betwixt Union and Confederate.

Sir, I am, and remain, your obedient servant. . .

Montgomery, Alabama
15 August 1861

Sir,

The journey has been pleasant, and I found comfortable accommodation which has greatly helped my recuperation from the experiences of the last ten days. Today is the 16th, and I am sufficiently refreshed to attend once more with vigour to the company's business.

First, with regards to this place: when I looked out of my bedroom window I could not help but see the grand dome, standing aloof, atop a public building. This reminds me of the dome of St Paul's Cathedral in London and made me feel quite homesick. I truly confess this is the first time such a thought has entered my mind, and the thought reinforced when I went for a walk about the city.

Yes sir, I can say with confidence this place of Montgomery has all the appearance and grandeur of a city, with its buildings and thoroughfares. The people are friendly, yet have a regal sedateness about them. To be truthful, this is my first encounter, since my landing on this continent, with what I consider to be a city. No small wonder that President Davis did select the capital of Alabama for his inauguration; there could be no finer a setting for such an auspicious occasion.

The population is large and the city established, unlike the capital of the Union which is in turmoil while it suffers its throes of expansion. The people here are well served by communications with the surrounding area and the east. Services could be improved if a forty to fifty mile length of rail link were laid from Selma, in the west: thus Montgomery would have the additional benefit of ready contact with New Orleans and Mobile. At present the port of Pensacola is the nearest, and the only one with a direct rail link to the city. I have been told the tale of the President's journey to this city for the historic event: because the aforementioned link was not in place, he and his entourage had an additional five hundred miles of journey.

The range of trade could increase twenty-fold if goods and produce could be transported readily and easily from the west by way of Vicksburg and Jackson. The same can be said of imports from the ports of New Orleans by way of Jackson; thus Jackson could be of importance to the company as a collection and distribution centre.

In my previous letters I commented on the Confederate rail network. Having travelled a reasonable section of the system, I can state with confidence that the whole system needs to be expanded. I was fortunate to have the opportunity to discuss this matter with the Mayor and elder dignitaries. It would seem there is a strong lobby for the government to take the lead in this matter. It is argued that the railway is a national asset, and as such should be protected by the people's representatives. Many see the government's role as one of coordination and planning.

My conclusion is that, with the proper dynamic leadership, the system could be raised to a high and efficient standard. Thus the riverways could convey merchandise to key staging-areas from whence the rail system could convey such items throughout the Confederacy. This should put them on par with the Union transport. Certain military gentlemen did convey to me the importance of an excellent river and rail network for the speedy transportation of troops and material to any point of crisis. If this argument holds good in war then equally it will hold good in times of peace.

For these reasons I would, sir, strongly recommend to you and the honourable members of the Board to grant me permission to set up an office here at the earliest opportunity. I propose to stay in this fair city until I receive a communication from you regarding the company's decision. My time will be put to good use, establishing contacts with individuals, organizations, groups and establishments with whom we can cooperate in various enterprises, investments and business.

Sir, with respect to the conflict, little appears to have been reported. News has arrived of a battle at Wilson Creek in

Missouri. The battle was part of the conflict I reported earlier, and this was one of the worst battlefields, so I have been informed, where a 150 foot spur of land known as Bloody Hill overlooks terrain of meandering streams, rocks and areas of bush. I was aghast to discover that the battle area measured no more than 520 yards by 175 yards. Into this went 14,000 Confederates under the command of General Price and Major General McCulloch, and 4,800 Unionists under General Lyon and Colonel Sigel. The Union force had been divided into two, Colonel Sigel leading 1,200 to flank the Confederate force.

The battle started when the Confederate camp was surprised by a bombardment from Colonel Sigel's force. Later the enemy forces came upon each other, both wearing grey uniforms. The Confederates were the first to realize the situation and charged; the Union force was routed. Then the whole force of Confederate troops turned to attack General Lyon's weak force.

The engagement on Bloody Hill has been described as bizarre: neither force could see the other due to the thick undergrowth. Each advanced, fired, then retreated to reload; no soldier could aim at a visible target. The battle on the hill raged fully five hours, during which time General Lyon was slain. Soon after, exhaustion overcame all participants. The Confederates held the field but sadly they seem to have lost the struggle for Missouri. The Union has appointed a governor and loyal state officials, as it occupies the capital of Jefferson City.

In terms of numbers the casualties were small: 1,317 on the Union side, of which 258 were dead. The Confederates suffered 1,336, including 281 dead. When these numbers are compared with the total numbers engaged, the losses represent a considerable percentage; some regiments on both sides were depleted by one-third. This surely demonstrates the savagery of the fighting: much was at stake and all seem to sense this.

Sir, I am, and remain, your obedient servant. . .

Montgomery, Alabama
1 September 1861

Sir,

I did receive your communication yesterday and have implemented the project.

There is a gentleman of excellent experience and character

who is keen to join the company's enterprise; I know I can leave the matter in his safe hands. He will communicate directly with me and for my part I shall inform you of progress. His name is Mr Wilbourforce.

On the matter of New York, may I enquire if you, sir, and the Board have yet reached a conclusion. This could be a missed opportunity if it is delayed. I will await the outcome of your deliberations, and know you will make a wise decision.

In the meantime I consider my business here to be concluded, and propose to take a train in two day's time for Columbus.

Sir, I am, and remain, your obedient servant. . .

Columbus, Georgia
4 September 1861

Sir,

The journey was relatively short and after obtaining accommodation, I have had time to walk about and note the populace and general disposition of the place, which lacks all the qualities of Montgomery, but is nevertheless pleasant.

The town, as I cannot judge it a city when compared with Montgomery, is astride but one rail track. Some fifty miles to the east the track divides in a north to south direction, the north leading to Macon, my next destination.

Columbus is close to the border with Alabama. The town boasts one reputable company, that of Louis Haiman and Brother, who fashion officers' swords, employing mainly German workers for their skills.

I did debate with the Mayor the possibility of linking with Montgomery in the common cause of trade; however, it was pointed out to me at great length that this would be impossible. Montgomery governs the State of Alabama, whilst Columbus is governed from Atlanta, the capital of Georgia, and never the twain shall meet. Each guards its own independence from invasion without, and especially from Richmond.

I did write at an earlier stage how things are viewed so differently on this continent. Each state is almost a separate nation, deciding its own contribution to the Confederacy. There is much confusion as to who commands the militia of each state on becoming part of the Confederate army. This state of affairs applies equally to the Union.

I cannot comprehend how the Union or the Confederacy

could possibly function should a state of war be declared, for not only can each state determine its quota of regiments, but each citizen has the right to enlist for short terms. I cannot see how either can ever hope to sustain a war under these various conditions. Hopefully these few engagements of arms, and the horror of the battles and injuries, will have a calming effect, and a force of arms will give way to sanity after those heady days of euphoria and glories of war have subsided.

While it may initially be a problem to have a base that serves various states, I feel that this is not a great hurdle to surmount; once acquainted with the laws and regulations of each state, it will be possible for the company to achieve interstate trading.

There is little else to keep me here so I shall spend another full day then depart for Macon.

Sir, I am, and remain, your obedient servant. . .

Macon, Georgia
7 September 1861

Sir,

As there is little here for me to observe, I intend to depart tomorrow for Atlanta, the capital of Georgia. My only three observations of this town are:

1 The town doth have a company, Spiller and Burr, who are makers of revolvers, unique in so far as they cover the iron breech with a portion of brass, This, so I'm told, has something to do with stresses at the moment of firing. I understand there are numerous arms' makers throughout this state.

2 Macon is astride the railway where there is a junction. (The railway plunges into oblivion in the south-west of the state.) Along this track is the branch to Columbus and Montgomery; a second branch from Macon drives east to the port of Savannah and the third branch thrusts north-west to Atlanta, Rome and Chattanooga. (What strange sounding names.)

3 Macon lies on the west bank of the Ocmulgee River, which flows into the Atlantic Ocean.

I have no proposal for Macon at the present time.

Sir, I am, and remain, your obedient servant. . .

Atlanta, Georgia
10 September 1861

Sir,

A pleasant day indeed when I arrived here.

My first impression is that this place has all the airs of being a capital: most business-like and well laid out. It lacks a little of the sedateness of Montgomery, but more than makes up for this minor defect with the enthusiasm for business.

15th September, and the time spent has been profitable.

Here are to be found the wealthy class, a middle class and the trades-working classes. The populace is reminded of the conflict through the newspapers which exude hell-fire in almost every issue, condemning the Unionists on every possible occasion. I am inclined to question the accuracy of these reports.

Inherent in all the classes is the spirit of the entrepreneur, so that it is not considered in bad taste to discuss business whenever and wherever the opportunity presents itself. I am truly impressed by the resourcefulness of individuals, in both their personal and business circumstances.

Two topics of conversation are generally encountered, one of which I have already touched upon. The second still relates to business but in the wider sense, namely the Confederacy. The good people are optimistic about their improved fortunes with the Confederacy compared to the restrictive, strangling conditions under the Union.

My conclusion is that it will be expensive to compete with a firmly established business community. However there may be fruitful prospects for the company should the policy be one of partnerships involving various selected businesses. I intend to explore discreetly and examine those companies that would match our trading principles, which task I estimate will take five to seven days to accomplish.

The good citizens are naturally concerned for the Confederacy and its relationship with the Union. They tend to dismiss the present series of armed conflicts as nothing unusual, confident that it has all been political manoeuvring for when the discussions begin. I did offer my considered opinion that the battle of Bull Run did not appear to have the hallmark of political manoeuvring. My acquaintances debated at some length why their opinion should prevail: the Union wished to establish a buffer zone on the south side of the River Potomac, while it was equally logical that the Confederacy desired to maintain a threat thus enabling it to negotiate from a position of strength.

I then did raise the matter of recent conflicts in the west. Again they had a perfectly logical explanation: the Union and Confederacy both desire, and consider it beneficial, for uncommitted states and territories ultimately to join them. Therefore it was to be expected that the two fractions within some of the states would try to settle the matter between themselves. West Virginia and Missouri were ideal illustrations for their argument. Although a Union governor at present administers in Jefferson City, and a provisional governor sits in Wheeling, in West Virginia, there is no guarantee this will remain so. Should President Lincoln adopt a belligerent and war-mongering attitude he may well come to regret his stance at the next election. There are still many people in the Union who desire peace not conflict. If war were truly to erupt then one would expect to see the Union peace movement swell, thus removing such a contentious president who seems intent on plunging the entire continent into an abyss to satisfy a personal, blinkered principle. A politician who boxes himself in is doomed to oblivion. These people seem confident that President Lincoln will be defeated at the next Union election, thus the Confederate has only to ride out the storm for the next few years and all will then be well.

22nd September. News has just reached Atlanta that a Union fort at Lexington, Missouri, was captured on 20th September and the garrison surrendered after eight days of attack. This would add substance to the view held by the people of this community.

My business is now concluded and I propose to say my farewells and depart tomorrow for Charleston. I am anxious to view the place since my previous visit: many consider this the birthplace of the Confederacy.

Sir, I am, and remain, your obedient servant. . .

Charleston, South Carolina
25 September 1861

Sir,

Since my last visit the port has undergone a marked change; the military is much in evidence, and although Fort Sumpter is functional once again and all the other forts have been strengthened, this change has overflowed into the port itself.

Citizens here know only too well that their action earlier this year has brought down on them the wrath of the Union. They pride themselves on having taken on the Union, showing the way for others, and liken themselves to the biblical hero of David, the Union as Goliath. I intend to stay only as long as it takes me to book a passage on a vessel to convey me to the port of Wilmington. This place is a hotbed of war activity, and I do not consider it a suitable atmosphere in which to conduct business whilst there remains a threat hanging over the place.

It is just conceivable that the Union may have plans to recapture Charleston for no other reason than the satisfaction of revenge, and does not intend this as an act of aggression against the Confederacy, but rather as retrieving what is rightfully its. Sir, I am, and remain, your obedient servant. . .

Wilmington, North Carolina
5 October 1861

Sir,

The trip proved to be both long and laborious; my first problem was in finding a vessel prepared to carry out the trip, as there was concern regarding Union warships on blockade duties off the coast. I begin to fear the good citizens were justified in their view of the Union intent. Finally, however, I found a captain, bolder than the rest, who considered it a challenge he would take pleasure in undertaking: it would be a pleasure to show those damn Yankees to be the fools they really are.

Naturally there was a price to be paid for his services on such a dangerous and arduous mission. Many times we had to run for shelter of an inlet whenever a ship was sighted. The captain was taking no chances; he had no wish to give those damn Yankees the satisfaction of capturing him.

Now I am arrived at this port and find its activities slow. This, I imagine, is due to the patrolling warships that have reduced commerce virtually to a trickle. There is nothing here to hold me and I have booked passage on a train for Petersburg early tomorrow morning.

One rail track goes north through Goldboro, then on to Petersburg and Richmond. Another track presses west, then turns north to Richmond; it also has branches to various places in South Carolina, including Charleston. I am able to stay aboard the good ship that did convey me here, to rest before the morrow.

May I respectfully request that if you, sir, have reached a decision regarding the New York proposal, you communicate this to my Richmond address where I expect soon to be.
Sir, I am, and remain, your obedient servant. . .

Petersburg, Virginia
9 October 1861

Sir,

This portion of the journey was indeed complex in the manner of the route taken, being an example of the result of various sections of track belonging to different owners. The track followed a tortuous route, crossing many rivers. The train trembled as it traversed each bridge, filling me with apprehension regarding the structural strengths of the various wooden assemblies. Surely with the considerable shaking each receives when a train does pass over it, the timbers are bound to split? How these trestle devices can withstand the battering of the elements and still remain standing is truly an engineering feat, especially when one is aware of the height to which some rise. I wonder about the effects of fire.

I intend to explore, and stay for a few days to recuperate before completing my rail journey.

14th October. Today I conclude this letter with a report of the place. Because of its close proximity to Richmond there seems little need to contemplate an office or base here: the area can adequately be served from Richmond, which is a mere twenty-five miles to the north. The town is served by four railways: to the south-east is the Norfolk and Petersburg track; to the west is the South Side track to Lynchburg; to the south is the Weldon track with spurs in various directions within the state of North Carolina; and to the north is the Richmond, Fredericksburg and Potomac track. This serves to illustrate well the subject of railways as detailed in my previous letters.

A tributary of the James River, the Appomattox, flows immediately to the north of the town, and many roads, dirt tracks in reality, radiate out of the town to the south in a veritable maze.

The town itself is based on a rectangular pattern. It boasts a courthouse, also a racecourse, the first I have encountered.

This graceful town, although the citizens do rebuke me strongly to call their city thus, has many a handsome building: the Cockade Monument for the men who died in the war of 1812; the Blandford church built in 1737 but abandoned in the 1800s; the Methodist and Presbyterian churches standing in Market Street, and A. L. Fittz, the tobacco auction house, which shares Sycamore Street with Mechanics' Hall, where children attend. This hall and St Paul's church nearby have a strong Greek style of architecture, as does the Petersburg Exchange on Bank Street, where farm produce is sold. The city has a tranquil atmosphere, almost that of a great park with the abundance of trees of many varieties.

Three homes worthy of mention are May House on the High Street belonging to John Fitzhugh, the elegant mansion built by Reuben Ragland in the 1850s in Sycamore Street, and the home of Francis Rives, in its spacious grounds on the corner of Market and Friend streets. These men belong to what are reputed to have been some of the first families in Virginia since the colonial days.

The river to the west side of Petersburg is in a rocky landscape and not deemed navigable; the covered Campbell Bridge allows workers access to the cotton mill. The bridge in the city centre provides access to Pocahontas on the north bank, where dwells a community of 3,000 free negroes – a most extraordinary contrast to the slave states in the Union and Confederacy. There is also the Bollings Dam on the river, which bears the name of another distinguished family.

This information I believe will demonstrate the value to the company of cultivating the friendship of these families, who are of importance and influence in this area. However, I see nothing to be gained at this time by setting up an office here, as the Richmond office is in close proximity, less than a day's ride on horseback

My long journey is almost concluded and I trust my letters have enabled you to visualise this land with its various manners, cultures, traditions and attitudes. I feel sure, sir, that you and the honourable members of the Board will share my belief that this land is worthy of the company's attention.

Tomorrow I shall ensure all is in order here before departing on the short journey north the following day.

Sir, I am, and remain, your obedient servant. . .

Petersburg, Virginia
15 October

My dearest mother,

My greeting to you, and I trust you enjoy good health and all is well on the estate. I was reminded of my birthplace when I visited some of the towns on my Odyssey of the Confederacy. But before I write of my experiences may I allay any fears you may have regarding the safety of my person. It is mainly the newspapers who carry stories of war so, mother dear, my advice is to treat them as works of fantasies.

Yes, mother it is true there have been a few conflicts. None on the grand scale of a war, and sadly, yes, lives have been lost and men wounded. The confrontations have been brief. I understand the purpose of them was to consolidate boundaries and to determine the loyalty and support of the uncommitted states.

Away from the two capitals nobody talks of war, all are interested in the future expansion of their areas and with it prosperity. The people talk of trade not war. So mother dear, do not worry about me, I am in no danger.

But now onto pleasurable matters. Let me tell you of the places I have visited on my journey through the Confederacy.

I did set out from Richmond at the beginning of July 1861 and expect to arrive back in Richmond on the 16th of October. Most of my journey was by train but on several occasions I did embark on ships to enable me to link one railroad to another. These voyages were of short duration and none involved going to sea, as each ship kept close to the shoreline, this being the quickest means of arriving at one's destination. Have no fear, mother, the masters of the vessels were extremely knowledgeable about the sea and currents in their areas. The trips were pleasant. Yes, there were occasions when Union warships were spotted, but the masters knew how to avoid them. I was sure no harm would come to me whilst in the safe confident hands of these old sea salts.

But I digress. My first stop was at Bristol, having passed through Lynchburg. The town is surrounded by many outlying communities who are served by these large and long wagons called prairie schooners. The area is mountainous, with many rivers, and it is a struggle against the land and weather to have a livelihood. The mayor fears it may become a ghost town as others have become.

My next stop was at a quaint place by the name of Chattanooga in the state of Tennessee. It is the centre for three railroads and nearby is the navigable River Tennessee. To the south are a number of towns but to the north only a few small settlements. It is a mountainous area with the town in the valley. I would describe the area as having the appearance of a stone-age scene.

Memphis, also in Tennessee, was next. It is a bustling port.To one side are a range of hills to protect the sprawling port with its scattering of imposing buildings, and beyond the town are numerous austere constructions where people of African origin live.

Alas, mother, I shall have to stop at this point to prepare for my journey to Richmond. I will write again as time permits.
Your loving son. . .

Six
Return to the Union

Richmond, Virginia
30 October 1861

Sir,

Since my arrival here on the 16th, I have found much business to attend to, this being the reason for the delay in writing.

The populace has indeed swollen from the original 40,000 souls since I departed in early July. People feel safer in the capital than in the surrounding areas, where many fear marauding Unionists. This is no small wonder after the Union intrusion at Bull Run and, I understand, the serious activities at the only other Union fort on Confederate soil.

The fort of Monroe is located at the mouth of the James River, on the north side, and faces across to the Confederate naval dockyards of Norfolk. 'Tis a most menacing Union outpost, as it is a mere eighty miles or thereabouts from Richmond which is also on the same river. Twenty miles to the north of the River James is the River York, flowing within twenty miles of the east of the Capital. Fortunately the Confederate military are well aware of this situation, and have in place counter-measures. I am disposed to think that Washington could also face a naval attack from the Potomac River. Thus, an impasse.

In view of the above, I did arrange a meeting with a representative from the office of General Lee, who is military advisor to the President. It is important to understand the structure of an army before one is able to appreciate the strategy of war. For a land of this dimension, speed of movement is an essential factor, crucial at the battle of Bull Run where the Confederates proved superior in transporting reinforcements quickly to the critical points. The railroad is the first factor, whilst knowledge of the terrain, thus avoiding a loss of time when units lose their way, is the second factor. As the gentleman remarked: 'An enemy who has you on the run will not oblige you by holding off while you bring up reinforcements.' This at least made sense to a mere lay person such as myself.

As to the army structure itself: it appears to be roughly based on the 'hundred unit', which helps with catering, clothing and supplies including munitions. I am informed that a hundred men from one town form themselves into a company with an officer in command, usually taking the rank of captain. One reason for such a number is to encourage local patriotism and pride, and to give comradeship and support in battle. This ploy, it is hoped, will overcome the problem of the short enlistment period presently operating.

When preparing for battle, it is convenient to group ten such companies into a regiment. It is conceded that the companies invariably will not be from the same area, or even from the same state. However, as each company is usually given its own objectives, to a degree each acts independently of the regiment in one sense, yet remaining part of the whole. Thus one or more companies can be detached during the development of a battle, which I am told happens quite often when for example, a flanking movement is deemed necessary, or to reconnoitre, intercept or block a retreat.

There are times when larger units are required by dictate of circumstances, and two to six regiments may form a brigade. Likewise three brigades may form a division, and two divisions a corps. I can only deduce two reasons for such large formations: to overwhelm an enemy or, more importantly, to enable large numbers to be moved to a given area as and when a threat arises. This saves time in repeatedly amassing the require numbers.

A cavalry company comprises more or less the same numbers as an infantry company, a regiment comprising of twelve companies. It seems that requirements to create larger units are not necessary. As to the artillery, these are considered as independent of the cavalry and infantry. A battery comprises six cannons and 144 men; between four and twelve batteries may form a brigade for the purpose of supporting an infantry corps.

I am afraid as a mere layman I cannot comprehend how cohesion is achieved in a battle when so many movements and counter-movements are made. I hope that some of my descriptions to date serve to illustrate the complexity of even a brief battle.

I did press my military companion as to how he perceived the differences between war in Europe and war in the Americas. He considered a number of factors to be changed since the Battle of Waterloo but did concede however, that many officers here are still educated in the battles of Europe, which remain their prime source of information. Many basics are still relevant even today.

Seldom has a European army had large numbers killed or seriously injured in hand-to-hand combat. My companion perceived that from the few conflicts to date, casualties occur at a distance from cannons, musket and rifles. This comes about from the great advances in design developments, leading to improved accuracy of weapons. When I enquired about the numbers of those killed or wounded here compared with those in Europe, the gentleman could not venture an opinion.

His view of the Confederate soldier compared with his European counterpart was thus: Europeans tend to be enticed into the army because of poverty or other pressing reasons, and remain because of the life, which in turn creates comradeship in arms and has even been known to extend to the enemy. In time many take pride in their regiment. Many English regiments are admired here for their past glories and reputations, many of which were experienced at first hand during the Independence conflict. He expected that a similar spirit would slowly manifest itself within Confederate companies, although its development is hampered by the short-term enlistment. Pride in a company is a temporary thing at present, and is the result of fellow-feeling between friends who join en bloc. The soldiers tend to have a fierce loyalty for state rather than companies. Companies come and go, states remain forever.

He said that there was little difference between the officer class in Europe and that in the Confederacy: for many such service is a family tradition. He did add that, should this become a war, then many families may well find one of their kin starting the tradition.

I did venture to ask the person concerned about the objectives of war and, put in simple terms, he said that when two European armies meet, it is a trial of strength and endurance, the victor enjoying the booty, usually land. The usual policy after victory is to permit conquered people to govern themselves in return for their agreement to become allies of the victor. This is usually acceptable to those of influence, while the peasants continue life more or less without change. History has shown that the peasants have witnessed many changes in those who govern. Naturally one must not forget that in every nation there are always zealous patriots and therefore, in the future, one must expect another trial of arms.

Here in the Confederacy, it is of prime importance to destroy the enemy force totally, to prevent its being a further threat. Part-destruction serves no purpose, it merely delays the determination of the outcome; thus supplies and transportation are important factors.

There is no army large enough on this continent, be it Union or Confederate, to occupy all the lands, therefore land is not the prime booty; rather it is the control of the land and the people that is of prime importance.

I did raise the matter of my recent tour, and how many of the populace of towns to the west were not the least concerned with the conflict in the east. In truth they did say that it was all the creation of foolish, blinkered politicians, who should know better. Nothing more than a storm in a tea cup. My companion did drily comment that the Boston tea party had been a storm. He also dismissed my observations, reminding me of the frailty of human beings. Many may debate the quantity of wealth and prosperity to be gained within a whole Union as opposed to that from a smaller and partial Union, but this is soon forgotten when a crisis occurs. Neutrality is no longer possible; reluctantly decisions have to be made. If right, the outcome will be success, but if wrong, then they reap disaster. I did interpose to ask why this is so, since such matters do not arise in Europe, and did provoke a sigh from him.

The truth of the matter is that Europe has a history that goes back thousands of years, whereas history is only beginning here. He further stressed that the Confederacy has yet to celebrate its first birthday. On this point the discussion ended. I had been greatly impressed, but am optimistic for the future of the Confederacy.

I did feel able to confirm the gentleman's observations regarding human beings and their reactions. The nearer to the east my journey has taken me, the more concern has been shown by the populace in general about the Union's intentions, instilling in them a determination to fight to the utmost to hold on to their gains. I found this particularly to be the case in Charleston, where the inhabitants were well aware of their prime importance in bringing about the present situation. Outwardly there was a great show of bravado, yet I sensed an inward fear of a wrathful retribution. Not until the Confederacy is truly established will they be released from their own Sword of Damocles.

Forgive the length of this letter, but there is much news to impart to you.

One matter that occurred in June I became aware of today. I

did mention the Union fort of Monroe; the new commander is none other than General Butler, the self-same General Butler who did of his own volition subdue the secessionists in Baltimore in May of this year. At the time of the June incident, the Confederate headquarters was at Yorktown, where the commander of a 2,500-strong force was General Magruder. He did send a regiment to Big Bethel; all the companies were from North Carolina under the command of Colonel Hill. The commander did well to prepare earthworks and timber defences, and position his 1,400 troops by 9th June.

Colonel Hill had his headquarters near the church. To his west were four companies manning an earthworks, while a further company held a wooded area to the north of this. Along north and east lines of the headquarters were three companies, and immediately to the south were two cannons. On the north bank of the River Back, to the east of the Yorktown road, were a company plus a cannon, then another company, these being of the Third Virginian infantry. To the west of the road was another company of the First Carolina infantry. Thus have I described this confined battle area with its woods and a marsh.

At 1 a.m. on 10th June, two columns from the fort of Monroe set forth to converge for a surprise dawn attack. One column comprised the Fifth New York, the Third New York and the Zouaves. The other column comprised the Seventh New York and parts of the First Vermont and Fourth Massachusetts; in all some 4,400 men.

Near the Confederates, the Unionists did mistake each other in the darkness and opened fire: twenty-one soldiers were killed or wounded. This alerted the defenders. Around 8 a.m. Union advance troops, I believe the military term is skirmishers, did drive back the Confederate skirmishers. The Unionists did then encounter the north-bank Confederate earthworks, whereupon the attackers were bombarded. Brigadier Pierce, who was leading the attack, did attempt flanking movements to the east and west, but the troops in the west flank attack were repulsed by heavy Confederate fire. On the east flank, due to the terrain, Union troops did mistake each other and fired so that each, fearing they were about to be themselves flanked, did withdraw. Another effort was made on the west flank. Companies of the Vermont and Massachusetts, under the command of Major Winthrop, tried to lead an attack during which the major was immediately slain. The troops became confused and withdrew in some disorder.

After two hours' fighting, the Union troops withdrew in a

bedraggled state to the fort from whence they had come. Fifty Unionists and ten Confederates lay terribly wounded, and there was a death toll of eighteen Unionists and one Confederate. Not surprisingly the two Union commanders lost their commands. This confirms my view that the Union is content to create buffer zones and nothing more.

Today, 1st November, I did receive your instruction regarding the New York project, and will depart forthwith to implement same, also to wait, with pleasure, the arrival of Mr Withring, the company's appointed representative.

Sir, I do not intend to write further until Mr Withring arrives.

Sir, I am, and remain, your obedient servant. . .

New York
5 December 1861

Sir,

Mr Withring did arrive a week ago, and the time has been spent acquainting him with the area. We have also acquired premises for the company, with accommodation for ourselves in the same building.

I have given Mr Withring details and information whereby he can conduct his own investigations with a view to completing a report of the results of his findings, views and recommendations. These I will send for your consideration along with my comments.

Should you, sir, require additional facts, costs or other information before submitting your report to the honourable members of the Board, I am sure Mr Withring and I will be able to furnish you with such items.

New York being a port, this did remind me to make inquiries on the matter of navies and possible blockades. The Confederate navy can rapidly be disposed of: it has some 237 officers, resigned from the Union navy, and a few cutters seized in April.

The Union fares a little better. It has 9,000 officers and ratings. On paper there are ninety ships, forty-eight of which are out of commission and in need of considerable repair. Of the remainder, thirty are old, sluggish, wooden-hulled sailing ships, and twelve are wooden-hulled steam cruisers. Most of these are in fact at present scattered around the world. The Union position is further plagued by the problem of protecting its vast merchant fleet which the Confederates could otherwise plunder at will. Because most of the Confederate trade is conveyed by foreign ships, this allows them the freedom to deploy their ships for other purposes. I understand from naval people that both sides appreciate the importance of a naval role, should the conflict become serious.

The first response of the Confederates has been to hire privateers to act in the name of the Confederacy, with the purpose of attacking Union ships. They had to keep within maritime law, which they did by stating that captured goods were contraband of war, thus permitting the privateers to sell them. A bounty of one-fifth of the value of the ship destroyed was to be paid by the Confederate government.

The Union countered this by claiming that such acts were piracy, and the guilty parties would be tried and, if convicted, hanged.

Now as to the maze of the legal situation: this seems to stem from a declaration in 1856, signed by England and France, that they would not accept privateering as a form of war. However, the then United States was not a signatory, and therefore retained the use of privateers, as have the Confederates, who deem themselves a nation, even though they are as yet not accepted by the nations of the world. Likewise, the Union could not declare a blockade unless it were prepared to recognize the Confederacy as a nation in its own right. I understand that International law defines a blockade as 'An act of war against a belligerent nation'. As it is likely to be a matter of time before the Confederacy is recognized as a nation, they can trade, raise loans abroad and buy arms if needs be. Are you, sir, aware of any such activity in England?

I see no reason to change my view that within a year or so the Union and the Confederacy will find the means of coexisting as two nations, in the same manner as the Union does with Canada. The information I have indicates that a Confederate commission has been active in seeking recognition by Her Majesty's Government, although there is a rumour that the commission has now been dissolved. Therefore I am confident from all the signs and happenings, and with the prevailing confusion over naval policy, that before any fruits are borne, it will be too late to impede the Confederates' advance to nationhood. If pursued with vigour, I can see no impediment to its achieving its goal by the end of 1862.

Regarding rumours, Mr Withring did say that privateers have been reported as being extremely active near New York and Boston. It has also been said that any disguised attempt at blockade by the Union cannot be successful, as the ships in question have to travel considerable miles to replenish, and thus could be off-station for a month or more. There have been certain occupations by the Union along the Confederate coastline, but these are of minor importance: with small garrisons, I see no reason why the Confederates will not retake them at their will. The forts of Clark and Hatteras, in North Carolina, were taken after a brief, yet vigorous, naval bombardment on 28th August. These forts were nothing more than log and sand in construction.

I was shocked to learn that Ship Island, between New Orleans and Mobile, was occupied by Union troops in early September, shortly after I had passed that way. I wonder what my fate, and that of the captain, would have been if passage had occurred during late September.

The forts of Walker and Beauregard, located at the entrance to Port Royal, which is a deep, inland natural harbour, were occupied after a brief naval bombardment. The port and forts are in South Carolina, between Charleston and Savannah. The Union's intention in obtaining these places is to provide depots to serve the unofficial blockading ships, thus time off-station is greatly reduced. There is also another depot off the south coast of Florida, called Key West. All this makes the navy's task that much easier. This is all I know to date regarding the respective navies and merchant shipping.

As to the land, there has not been a great deal happening. What I am able to report might not be in strict chronological order due to the manner of receiving the information.

There appears to have been a pointless confrontation at Belmont, near Columbus in the state of Missouri, close to the border with Kentucky. The Union troop, 3,114 strong, left its base in Cairo on the Mississippi River under the command of General Grant. The battle commenced at 8 a.m. on 7th November. Opposing the Union force was Brigadier General Pillow with 2,700 men. The battle did sway back and forth until finally the Confederate force broke. General Polk, in Columbus, did fire upon the Union force and sent a force to cut the enemy off from its boats. This objective, however, was not achieved, and resulted in some 600 casualties on each side. General Grant withdrew to Cairo, moving thence to occupy Paducah, on the Ohio River, some twenty-five miles to the east. I understand that General Fremont was overall Union commander in the area, General Johnston being in command of the Confederates.

Both sides are engaged in recruitment in Kentucky, while the

Confederates are also seeking men from Tennessee, Arkansas and Mississippi. It seems as if two great armies are forming in Kentucky, held to be a crucial state and much prized by both sides.

There was further movement along the Potomac River during September and October. General J. Johnson, not to be confused with General S. Johnston in Kentucky, did commence on 27th September to reform his 41,000 army into a defensive triangle, the tip at Centreville and its base from Manassas to Bull Run. This was completed by 17th October. This did prompt a reaction from the Union commander, General McClellan, who did instruct the occupation of Munson Hill and Fairfax Court House, vacated by the Confederates. Then on 19th October, Brigadier General McCall with 13,000 troops did enter Dranesville, from where he was to conduct a reconnaissance. This movement was intended to remove the Confederates from Leesburg without actual battle. To further this objective, General McClellan did order Brigadier General Stone to move across the Potomac and demonstrate his strength in such a manner as to encourage the enemy to withdraw, the threat of McCall and Stone together hopefully achieving the right response.

One of Stone's patrols reported a small Confederate camp at Balls Bluff which McCall elected to attack the next day. He would establish a bridgehead on the south bank of the Potomac, directly opposite Leesburg. Stone was to take a force of 300 men and cross at Balls Bluff, further upriver. Reinforced with a further hundred men he did advance but found no camp, so marched on to Leesburg, where the Confederate Colonel Evans had moved 2,000 troops to counter McCall's threat at Dranesville. Small forces from both sides discovered each other outside Leesburg, and the battle commenced.

Colonel Evans sent a regiment to hold Stone, dispatching the rest of his force to counter the Unionists near Leesburg. Colonel Deven was forced to retreat to Balls Bluff where the final fight took place. I understand Colonel Evans had placed his troops in a better position than Colonel Deven's, although the point of victory for the Confederates came about by a freak misunderstanding. A mounted officer did rein up before the Union lines and ordered an advance, resulting in the Union troops being cut to pieces by the heavy fire from the Confederates; hence their retreat off the bluff and to the Potomac. It would seem that the officer was a Confederate who had mistaken the Union troops for his own side. Likewise, the Union soldiers had mistaken the officer as one of theirs. The frightful slaughter came when the

Union troops had the choice of dying where they stood, surrendering, or taking their chances and falling over the deep and rocky bluff to the river's edge far below. Many died in the fall, and many others drowned as the result of failing to discard their heavy equipment; others died from the continuing enemy fire.

In the meantime McCall had completed his objectives and withdrawn for Dranesville. Had communications been effective his force, and that of McCall at the bridgehead, might well have saved the day. Equally, the poor planning of the two river crossings by a few boats did hamper any swift movement of large numbers across the Potomac. Added to this was the lack of communication from and to Colonel Deven; the disaster for the Unionists was complete.

Back in Washington there was much fury at this defeat, with many demanding further action to vindicate the Union army. At the end of that day 529 Union soldiers had been taken prisoner. Forty-nine bodies were found on the battlefield and 198 were wounded. It was estimated that a further hundred drowned in the retreat. The Confederates lost thirty-six dead, 117 wounded and two missing. The Union losses were not justified for an action that was never planned, and from which nothing was gained. President Lincoln's long-time friend, Colonel Baker, did lose his life in the fight.

I will conclude this letter as I wish to make preparations to be in Washington for the rest of the month. My purpose is to seek information regarding Union policy for 1862.

Sir, I am, and remain, your obedient servant. . .

Washington
31 December 1861

Sir,

Since arriving in the capital I have found matters extremely secretive, but there is evidence all around from military activities, to suggest that something is about to happen. One possible answer is the fear that the capital may be captured. To this end a great many fortifications, a veritable network of them, have sprung up, stretching for many miles. This would at least justify the large concentration of troops. McClellan was appointed Commander-in-Chief on 1st November to replace the elderly and extremely experienced Winfield Scott, a hero of the Union after the Mexican war.

One final clash took place near Dranesville on 20th

December, when two brigades did encounter each other head-on. The Confederates had the worst of the encounter, with almost 200 killed and wounded compared with sixty-six on the Union side. With the end of this year, it would seem that the Union forces in the east and west are in a paralyzed state, most of their sorties coming to nothing.

The atmosphere in the capital has changed. There is now unease: nothing has been resolved since April when the expectation of the people was that it would all be over in six months, the matter settled by arms, determining whether the erring states would once more be part of the Union or finally go their own way.

I also sense a general feeling of distrust within certain classes, since some eminent persons were arrested for spying. No doubt Richmond also has its quota of spies. When I passed through Washington from Richmond earlier, I did find the guards on the Potomac bridge friendly, yet vigilant, as if expecting the appearance of greycoats at the southern end of the bridge at any moment. I wonder what I shall find on my return to Richmond tomorrow.

Sir, on Christmas Day I did attend church to offer prayers for you and your family and for the members of the Board. My special prayer is for this continent: that there will be no more bloodshed and that people shall talk unto people, and that politicians shall heed the people's cry.

This New Year's Eve I feel will be marked in history as a momentous point in time. Will peace and common sense prevail? I sincerely hope so, for otherwise many people will feel the finger of tragedy touch them. Civil war is a bloody and barbarous enterprise from which it takes one or more generations to heal the rifts and bitterness.

Sir, I conclude this, my last letter for 1861, with good wishes and the hope of wealth and happiness for all those in England. Sir, I am, and remain, your obedient servant. . .

Seven
Towards nationhood

Richmond
5 January 1862

Sir,

Greetings on the start of a new year. I can report that all is generally well.

My journey from Washington was uneventful. The guards on the bridge did examine all those who crossed, no matter from whence they came. I was treated with friendliness and courtesy; they did not delay me long, and were particularly pleasant when they discovered I was from England.

I have yet to study the reports and information that have been accumulating since my absence, and will send you my report soon. In the meantime I have only one item of usefulness, relating to the matter of privateers. It would seem that the Union occupation of certain coastal areas has resolved the thorny legal question as to the validity of such privateers. Their ships need deep-water anchorages from which to off-load and sell their contraband, of which facilities they have now been deprived by Union action. Further, they can no longer dispose of the contraband in English ports; there have been no reports of privateer activity since Christmas. There is rumour that shallow-draft vessels, seen in many Confederate ports, have evaded the Union ships on their blockade duty.

Although I am no military person, I feel I can safely say that the war, as such, in 1861 was almost non-existent. Yes, there was one major clash at Bull Run, involving relatively large forces, but I do put this down as being no more than a test of each side. The Union wishes to create buffer zones to protect their capital since the capture of Washington might well split asunder the people's resolve. The peacemakers and subdued secessionists may well be in the ascendancy should the unthinkable happen.

For the Confederate military, they seem more content to build and defend. Their confidence has risen a great deal as the result of the many minor confrontations to date. They are quick to point out that this means the necessity of vigilance at all times, and the readiness to move without hesitation to counter any threat, intended or real, that the Union may devise.

The Confederate administration and military appear to be in accord regarding the dubious attempts to blockade, confident that these will dissipate during the course of this year as the blockade-runners become skilled. For this reason they do not intend to wrest back those coastal areas presently seized, which at present serve as fuelling points for the meagre Union fleet. There should be some booty for the Confederates when such places are abandoned, once the Union realizes the futility of such a secretive and illegal policy.

The first five days of this year may prove a good omen. This could be the testing year of the Confederacy, if it hopes to survive and become a proper nation in the near future. Once the Confederacy is established, the Union government, particularly President Lincoln, will have to abandon its present declared intent of bringing the Confederate states back into the Union.

Examining the conflicts I have described to you over the past year has brought to my notice one important fact. With the exception of Bull Run, a special case, and the army action along the coast, all other clashes did not take place on Confederate soil. In reality these clashes were for the souls of key uncommitted states, the greater number occurring in the state of Missouri. One fact does disturb me relating to the clashes themselves: from the figures I have quoted you, it will be noted that adding together the total number of combatants and then adding together the numbers of dead and wounded, the comparison between the two sums is alarming. Approximately one-third do become casualties of this so-called war. If there were to be several battles involving large numbers, and each were fought with the same ferocity as presently reported, then I fear a decimation of mankind for both nations. Can either side truly take this step, and then justify a war of such type and magnitude?

I trust the above may allay any foreboding on your part, sir, or any of the honourable members of the Board. Nevertheless I shall remain vigilant for signs to the contrary that may be harmful to, or not in the interest, of the company. It is my intention to instruct the other company representatives in this land to report any incident, no matter how trivial, to me instantly. Thank goodness for the foresight of those who constructed the

railways, especially that marvel of speedy communication, the telegraph, which stands alongside the rail-tracks. Messages that can transverse long distances in a matter of minutes must surely be a miracle.
Sir, I am, and remain, your obedient servant. . .

Richmond
1 February 1862

Sir,
I have today received an excellent report from Mr Withring and similar confident expectations from the other representatives to the west. These I shall place before you, in their original entirety.

January did produce two incidents which I shall forthwith relate to you, the first associated with the Union coastal policy.

Brigadier General Wise has been urging Richmond to reinforce the island of Roanoke, at the estuary to the ports of Elizabeth City and Plymouth. The commander for the area, Major General Hugar, has declined to release reserve troops. The defences of the island appear to comprise 3,000 troops. There are three forts: Barstow, Blanchard and Huger, along the west coast, with twenty-five guns. A strong point of seven guns on a barge commands the western channel, which has been blocked by wrecks and pilings. On the east shore there are two guns at Ballast Point, which is low marshy terrain. The major obstacle for an invading force is in the narrow central area of the island where there is a redoubt, eighty feet wide, with one central and two end guns, and 1,000 troops. Trees for 700 yards have been felled to give a good field of fire, while either side of the redoubt are cypress swamps, almost impossible to traverse. In addition there are eight small boats, each armed with one gun.

Rumours abound that a large Union naval force with considerable transports is en route to the island. Indeed the newspapers have carried daily reports on the progress of the force, which seems to have been assembling at Annapolis, in Maryland, since early January. Another report stated that the steamer *City of New York* did founder in the inlet of Hatteras on 13th January. It was laden with guns, ammunitions and supplies to the value of $200,000. This seemed to indicate the size and serious intent of the Union force. The newspapers have even been able to name the Union commander as Brigadier General Burnside, ridiculed for his past command at Bull Run where the First Rhode Island regiment fought. However, after their ninety-day enlistment period expired most went home, leaving the General with no regiment to command. Gleefully, many folk anticipate that after Burnside's expected second defeat, the same will happen again within the Union regiments.

I did write to you of General S. Johnston and his defensive preparations for Nashville, Tennessee, a line stretching from Columbus, with General Polk's troops in the extreme west of Kentucky, and the construction of the forts Henry and Donelson, north-west of Nashville. Then to the north Brigadier General Buckner did occupy Bowling Green, while to the east Brigadier General Zollicoffer did fortify the Cumberland Gap, in a mountainous region close to the River Cumberland. Major General Crittenden was appointed as superior officer to Zollicoffer, and decided to attack a large Union force under the command of General Thomas. On the night of 18th January the Confederate force of 4,000 troops did march through rain and mud and next morning, although exhausted, did battle with a Union force of equal size. This fight did rage back and forth during a thunderstorm. The Unionists held strong positions, and their troops had been well rested before the encounter. In the confusion, at one stage of close-quarter combat, Zollicoffer mistook a Union officer as one of his own, and was shot dead for his mistake. Sadly the Confederates' arms were of poor quality and the wet hampered the functioning of the many flintlocks that used priming-powder, thus they finally had to retire in the face of a bayonet charge and a hail of bullets. This clash at Mills Springs did weaken Johnston's line in the east.

It did come to me, while writing reports of these conflicts, that a map would be of use to you. Therefore, sir, I am sending you one at the earliest possible moment.

Mills Springs is in Kentucky, which is not Confederate soil. I do not consider the situation has changed from my previous observations.

Sir, I am, and remain, your obedient servant. . .

Richmond
1 March 1862

Sir,

The Union has developed a new weapon of war: a metal-constructed ship with various guns as armament. It is claimed that few shore guns can damage these vessels.

In the meantime news has arrived in the capital regarding

Union activity in the west. General Fremont has been recalled to Washington and his command divided. I am not sure if this is a good or bad sign. Divided is weakened, but divided also means that vigilance needs to be doubled. Kansas is to be commanded by Major General Hunter; Arkansas and western Kentucky to be commanded by Major General Halleck. Brigadier General Buell replaces Sherman in Ohio, while General Grant commands the troops in Cairo as part of Halleck's force. Grant's force has been increased to 20,000.

On 6th February 17,000 Union soldiers were landed near Fort Henry, one group under General Smith to capture the high ground across the Tennessee River; the second group under Brigadier General McClernand to advance on the fort. In the meantime, seven gunboats directed at the fort a continuous bombardment. The Confederate General Tilghman realized the odds and, wishing to sustain the least amount of losses in his command, left a token force to oppose the gunboats and withdrew 2,500 troops to Fort Donelson. Later that day the few left in the fort surrendered.

The fort could not seriously be considered as important, being mainly earth in construction and under water for parts of the time. The interesting factor to emerge from the two-hour duel of guns was that the iron-clad gunboats were not invincible: serious damage was inflicted on two of the vessels. Not unexpectedly the nearby Fort Donelson remained a threat to the Union; however, there was no immediate attack. Grant was waiting for reinforcements of 10,000 troops, and the gunboats had first to return to Cairo for repair, then to sail up the Cumberland to where Fort Donelson is situated.

In the meantime, Johnston and his second-in-command General Beauregard did meet in Bowling Green to confer. Johnston decided on a withdrawal from Bowling Green and sent Beauregard to take charge of the withdrawal of Polk's force from Columbus. Johnston remained to attend the withdrawal of Major General Hardee's force.

At Fort Donelson, the 5,000 troops were commanded by three brigadiers: Buckner, Pillow and Floyd. The position seemed strong. The fort was in the form of a semi-circle: the south end near the river, the north end protected by a deep swamp. The river was overlooked by two batteries of guns on high ground. Grant approached the fort at dusk on 12th February with 15,000 troops and summoned up a further 2,000 from Fort Henry. The battle order next day was for General Smith to be on the left with Brigadier General McClernand to the right, to close off a Confederate escape route. This was not achieved: the weather suddenly intervened with freezing temperatures and a cold drizzle. Many troops on both sides were unprepared for this sudden change and suffered greatly because of inadequate clothing. They could not light fires since these invited the bullet speeding from out of the darkness.

On that day General McClernand did attack some guns with three regiments. This failed, incurring many casualties, some of whom were incinerated in fires caused by cannon igniting leaves and grass, while those who survived the fires froze to death. What a gruesome fate for the poor devils.

At 3.30 p.m. on the 14th, Grant received the 10,000 reinforcements. At the same time, the fleet of six ships closed on the fort and commenced firing. The fort guns waited until the ships came closer; the Union ships were thoroughly beaten. The commander of the ships, Foote, thought to repeat the success of Fort Henry by going close. However, in this situation, the guns would better have been deployed from a distance; at close range they proved ineffectual.

Johnston had by this time regrouped his forces near Nashville, and the plan was now to break out of the fort and join the main army at Nashville. Pillow's Confederates did attack McClernand on the right, by the river, and after a struggle put the Union front to disorderly flight. I understand that the rest of the Union front remained idle, having been instructed by Grant, before he left the headquarters on a visit to Foote, not to provoke any action. As no one was able to locate the commander for new orders, most felt helpless. Finally a brigade was sent by Wallace, but on the way they did fire by mistake on some of their own troops who were attempting a rearguard action. Grant was finally alerted to the breakout; Wallace and McClernand were to regain the ground lost, made possible because, for some unexplicable reason, at the moment of triumph Pillow withdrew to the fort. In the meantime Smith did attack the Confederates to the right and after a brief fight did capture and hold the earthworks. The next day most of the force found an escape route, leaving Buckner to surrender the fort. Union claims were in excess of 12,000 prisoners and a great host of material. This claim I suspect is extremely inaccurate: I do believe the figures of 450 dead and 1,500 wounded on the Confederate side, 500 dead and 2,100 wounded on the Union side.

For this engagement Grant was promoted to Major General. For some reason best known to the Union, there were many celebrations for taking Fort Donelson, which to me was but a minor victory, and not even truly that, since it was made easier by the Confederate withdrawal and surrender. Shortly after, the 45,000-strong Union force commanded by General Buell did occupy the recently vacated Bowling Green. They advanced and took Nashville within hours of Johnston's withdrawal.

It is perhaps understandable why the battles at the two forts may be viewed as being of little importance, as they were on the border with the unaligned state of Kentucky. But these positions were conceived as part of the defence line, to protect not only Nashville, but the entire state of Tennessee. Worse, this is a blow to the Confederates, as Nashville is the capital of the state and thus the first to be occupied by the Union, which must surely boost their morale. If the three forces of Major General Dorn in Arkansas, Beauregard and Polk in western Kentucky, and Johnston in north Alabama were to counter, then the loss could be recovered. Nashville is not only a capital; of major importance is its industry and armament production.

The long-predicted landing at Roanoke Island did take place on 7th February. 10,000 were landed approximately half way along the west side of the island, and the next day did advance in three columns: one column to mount a direct assault on the fortifications while the other two columns were to progress on either flank, taking them through some terrible terrain. Union gunboats commenced bombarding Fort Barstow. The small vessels of the Confederates did attempt to decoy the enemy towards the guns of Forts Hugar, Blanchard and Forrest. This failed, and two of their boats were damaged.

On the Confederates' right, the Union troops penetrated the obstacles and charged the fortifications, causing the smaller Confederate force to retreat.

In the centre two assaults had failed, but the third did succeed; however, the Confederates had withdrawn beforehand. Many of the 2,500 Confederate prisoners were paroled and a small number escaped. Twenty-three Confederates were been killed and fifty-eight wounded. The Union suffered thirty-seven dead and 214 wounded. Within hours the island was in Union hands.

Here in Richmond the blame was apportioned to General Hugar and the secretary of War, Mr Benjamin.

The final act was to take place further upriver near Elizabeth City, where fourteen Union gunboats did battle with the six remaining vessels of the Confederate force. Only one Confederate vessel did escape, the remainder were destroyed. Sadly, it was truly a David-and-Goliath confrontation, but this time David did not have a suitable sling. On 10th February the Union troops did occupy Elizabeth City.

Sir, I feel that although the greater portion of my letter includes details of conflicts as and when I receive them, I do consider them to be of prime importance to the company. They do provide the background to any trading we shall do, be it north or south. Please inform me if you wish the war reports to be discontinued.

Sir, I am, and remain, your obedient servant. . .

Richmond
30 March 1862

Sir,

I did receive your communication and note that you wish me to continue the reports. I am a little uncertain as to the intent of either side in this argument, for as yet, I cannot comprehend that all that has taken place to date can be considered a war.

On 14th March the Union forces moved further inland to an important rail junction of New Bern. Again Burnside did deploy three columns: Foster on the right, Parke in the centre and Reno on the left. The Confederate Brigadier General Branch had constructed earthworks, and used Fort Thompson as part of the defence line. The Union fleet did bombard from the River Neuse, but did bring Foster's advance to a halt when the shells landed among the Union troops. Reno's force did charge a brickworks at the railway tracks and drove out the Confederate defenders. Shortly afterwards they in turn were driven out by a Confederate counter-attack. Reinforcements from the centre did restore the situation, and at this point, with their defences broken and short of ammunition, the Confederates did withdraw to New Bern before falling back to a new line of defence.

This battle manoeuvre, known as flanking, seems to be used whenever possible: surprise and greater strength usually win the day. However, my military friends do warn me that this flanking by one side can mean defeat for them should the other side hold, then in turn attack and force a retreat. Methinks it is all a matter of luck.

At New Bern the Confederates suffered sixty-four dead, 101 wounded and 413 missing, the Union ninety dead and 380 wounded. Again there were 4,500 Confederates to oppose 11,000 Unionists and thirteen warships.

On 8th March a naval battle commenced at Hampton Roads,

a wide shallow channel, eight miles long, where three rivers join to empty into Chesapeake Bay, an area that threatens both capitals.

Apart from the *Merrimac*, a mighty Confederate ironclad, the remainder of the Confederate navy was positioned in the James River.

The events leading to this confrontation started on 6th March, when the Union ironclad left New York to take up duties in the Potomac in order to protect Washington. In the meantime the *Merrimac* left Gosport to engage the Union fleet, its prime target. To take on seventeen ships seems to me to be an indomitable task, but nevertheless that is what happened.

The first target was the twenty-four-gun sloop *Cumberland*, which was rammed. The bizarre incident reminded me firstly of the Roman-style galleys with their awesome, menacing rams, and secondly of a bee, when the *Merrimac* left its ram embedded in the side of the luckless sloop. It sank with the loss of 121 crew, all dead. Next came the fifty-gun wooden-hulled *Congress*, which was blasted then fired. Now it was the turn of the forty-gun *Minnesota*, which had unfortunately run itself aground and presented a bulky sitting target. However an ebb tide and darkness intervened.

The *Merrimac*, with two guns disabled and a riddled smoke-stack, retired to prepare for the next day. Two of the crew were dead and nineteen injured, including the captain. By the evening of 8th March the *Monitor* had arrived, after nearly sinking in bad weather en route. This ironclad was small compared to the mighty *Merrimac* and worse, had only two guns. The scene was now set for the morrow, the first task for the small ironclad being to protect the stranded *Minnesota*.

At six minutes past eight that morning the *Merrimac* fired the first shot at the *Monitor*. Thereafter for the next four hours each manoeuvred and exchanged shots from as close as ten yards to half a mile apart. Unlike the sailing ships, both ironclads could move and turn more quickly. The *Monitor* was the faster and offered the smaller target, but took eight minutes to load and fire its two guns, whereas the *Merrimac* could load its ten guns in five minutes. The *Monitor* had the advantage of a shallow draft, being well suited to the area, whereas care had to be taken to prevent the *Merrimac* from running aground, particularly in an ebb tide. I understand at one point it did indeed strike a sandbank and took fifteen minutes to get clear. With powder running short, the *Merrimac* tried to ram the *Monitor*, which nevertheless was able to slip aside.

Past noon and the captain of the *Monitor* lay injured, but the vessel had managed to slip away from its foe.

The *Merrimac* assumed that the *Monitor* had given up, so with limited ammunition it elected to finish the *Minnesota*. The Union ship had luck on its side that afternoon, helped by the tide. The *Merrimac* sailed for home.

I understand that tales and discussions about the two-day battle at sea, not far from either capital, did continue for a long time afterwards.

Sir, I fear that 9th March 1862 will go down as a black day in the history of human beings. On that momentous day, many did witness an event played out on the high seas between two weird-shaped, awesome creatures, the creations of human mind and ingenuity: two armour-clad vessels that can actually float, and can deliver devastating, destructive power against any fort, land defences, or batteries of the mightiest cannons.

The wooden-hulled warship has no answer to this challenge. Were several such warships with fifty cannon apiece to encounter one of these metal monsters, grounded due to engine or steering failure, even then the wooden-hulled warships could not destroy it as was witnessed on 9th March. If two such inventions did battle with one another and neither could destroy the other, then the facts would speak for themselves. I cannot believe that man's ingenuity will find a way to defeat these creatures for many years to come, and my fear is that this will not deter the Confederate or Union from rushing to create more of these terrible machines of war. Imagine the fate of a luckless wooden ship, were it to encounter such a weapon: in the blinking of an eye, Davey Jones's locker would receive another vessel of death.

My greatest fear stems from my tour of the Confederacy. Having seen all those communities that have the misfortune to have been built near the water, I can picture them lying in a heap of smouldering remains, razed to the ground by a spiteful bombardment from one of those monsters.

It did occur to me that I wrote previously of ironclad vessels being employed to attack forts. These vessels have sheets of metal covering an existing framework which can be damaged and destroyed. However, the *Merrimac* and the *Monitor* are designed and specially built to a careful specification with due care to armaments and their functions. The other major factor is that they are plated with specially-made armour, many inches thick. The appearance of these two vessels I liken unto Pandora's Box. How soon will it be before all the navies of the world have such ships, and knowing man's propensity for such things, devise even greater, totally invincible ships?

News has just reached me regarding General Jackson, the Confederate commander, who has been based at Winchester in an area known as the Shenandoah Valley, in West Virginia. Opposing him has been the 18,000-strong Union army of the Valley, commanded by Major General Banks, whilst in west Virginia, across the Alleghennies, there were 22,000 troops under Brigadier General Rosecrans and Brigadier General Kelley, with 5,000 troops positioned in the village of Romney, some forty miles from Winchester.

Information given me by a military adviser did indicate that although Jackson's force was small in number, he nevertheless intended to attack. The plan was to lull the Union into thinking that General Johnston had sent troops from his Manassas-Centreville army to reinforce Jackson's force. This would lure McClellan to attack the supposedly weak Johnston, whereupon Jackson would speedily join Johnston to defeat the Union and then return to occupy north-west Virginia.

Jackson was joined by Brigadier General Loring, the total force now numbering 7,500 volunteers, 2,200 militia and 650 cavalry. The small force did set out on New Year's Day, and early in January forced 1,400 Unionists to abandon Bath. There was a report that certain commanders were timid in the execution of their orders and thus the enemy force was allowed to withdraw intact. On 13th January the Union troops abandoned Romney, fearful of confronting a large Confederate force. Jackson had achieved his first objective: that of removing the threat to Winchester. He returned to his headquarters leaving troops in Romney, Bath and Martinsburg.

Rumour has it that conflict between officers and the commander did cause problems in Richmond, but finally the matter appeared settled. It then seemed that Johnston did move south on 7th March, provoking an advance of the Union forces including those under Banks's command who had occupied Winchester the day after Jackson had left.

Jackson's aim was to keep Banks occupied in the Valley so that he would not cross the Blue Mountain and flank Johnston's forces on the other side of the mountains. Banks in fact was sending regiments out of the Valley, leaving behind one large force of about 10,000 at Winchester. Brigadier General Shield expected Jackson to move on Winchester, and prepared for him at Kernstown. Shield had been alerted by an all-day skirmish south of Winchester, on 22nd March. Thus half his force prepared near Kernstown while another force waited north of Winchester.

On Sunday afternoon, 23rd March, Confederate guns opened fire. A small force of Confederates did demonstrate before the strong part of the Union line, whilst Jackson's main force attacked the weaker part of the line. All went well for a time. Shield, realizing what was happening, sent reinforcements to strengthen the weak sector. The battle raged for two hours, with wave after wave of Union troops charging the Confederates. Sadly the Confederates had to withdraw when their ammunition became low. Jackson suffered 718 casualties, the Union 590.

Unbeknown to Jackson, his daring to attack made the Union command revise its strength in the Valley. Banks's troops, who had left the Valley, were immediately returned, plus a further 9,000 troops. In western Virginia, a further 10,000 troops were sent to bolster Major General Fremont's force. Because of both Johnston's and Jackson's activities, Washington was also concerned about the capital itself: thus 40,000 were held to man the capital's defences. A further 25,000 were sent to bolster the force at Manassas.

Thus, sir, I have reported all movements that have come to my notice. It would seem that these activities are causing confusion for the Union and could well disrupt whatever plans they may be preparing. Any delay bodes well for the Confederates.
Sir, I am, and remain, your obedient servant. . .

Eight
The two fronts of Virginia

Richmond
30 April 1862

Sir,

Most of my letter, sadly, relates to the conflicts of this past month. These I shall endeavour to chronicle for you. Before I begin to detail the clashes, I do feel a personal observation is in order. When I first arrived on this continent, I commented upon the vastness and the impression of unending space, further reinforced by my two rail trips and several brief excursions. The mystery for me is how two forces can actually meet in the first instance: in the open spaces there is little by which the forces can navigate with certainty. Thus I would expect that on many occasions the opposing sides in fact pass within a few miles of each other, neither being aware of the other. This matter has been illustrated by regiments losing their way, yet fortuitously arriving at an opportune and critical point in the battle, their only compass being the sound of warfare and, I suspect, reaching the spot more by luck than judgment. It must be a problem to a commander to prepare battle plans that invariably require the time factor to enter into the design.

The terrain of this vast land has also amazed me, as the landscape changes so unexpectedly: it is possible to stumble into an impassable, or near impassable area when you are least expecting it. Thus it seems that most of the battles are played out on terrible terrain. These areas of death do not have comparisons in Europe. The battlefields of the past, in England and Europe generally, are such large open areas as to enable opposing armies to be arrayed in their full strength within sight of the enemy. I do understand that a show of strength has been known to weaken the resolve of one side, but this technique of intimidation fails to be effective here: many times a

Confederate force is outnumbered but will continue to fight until fate decrees otherwise.

The Confederate have the skill of selecting their battle-grounds, a skill understood by good army commanders in Europe. Sadly, a woeful shortage of men and equipment means that invariably they are unable to exploit their skills to maximum effect.

While writing this letter it did come to me that perhaps it is possible for two groups to engage if they employ cavalry as scouts. However I see a flaw in this: those on such an errand would need to have some personal knowledge of the local terrain. It must be a calculated gamble on the part of a commander to rely on information from local inhabitants. The general opinion from the military of both sides is that the size and identity of the opposing force can only be guessed at. Further, it is almost impossible to learn quickly about any movements of regiments in the battle; couriers are still the favoured method for this.

Perhaps ignorance of opposing numbers is a blessing; otherwise who knows what fearful thoughts may enter a man's mind as he prepares for battle. The logistics must also be a daunting and demoralizing challenge, since wagons are the prime means of transport and river transport has geographic limitations.

These facts demonstrate the immense difficulties and pressures that make it impossible for the whole thing to be sustained: sooner or later the combatants will become exhausted. Past history of wars has shown this every time.

Sir, now to the matter of this letter.

The Union General-in-Chief McClellan did attempt a two-pronged attack, one directed towards Winchester, the other towards Evansport. This was aborted because the barges required were unable to pass through locks, as they were six inches too big. So much for the planners of destruction. Had these two attacks materialized the Confederates no doubt would have been the victors, but the hand of fate decreed otherwise, and so the Confederates had to face a stronger challenge.

In the meantime Richmond's attention seems to have been diverted by an atmosphere of distrust between President Davis, Commander-in-Chief Johnston, and Secretary-of-War Mr Benjamin. Johnston did withdraw his 42,000-strong army from Manassas, and pass near Blue Ridge Mountains to the River Rappahannock, north of Richmond. The Union newspapers ridiculed McClellan for his timidity in failing to take advantage of this withdrawal. The Confederates had won the bluff on two counts. First, they had created the impression they had 150,000 troops at Manassas, and secondly, with the aid of dummy guns made of wood, they managed to delay the Union occupation of the abandoned defences and any pursuit thereafter.

A pursuit would have resulted in vast numbers of Confederates being killed or left behind. I can only surmise that time was a deciding factor for the Confederates. However, Johnston had prevented an outflanking movement by McClellan. Further, nature now conspired against the Union army, making it difficult to the highest degree to continue to advance along the tracks that had been turned into mud morasses and to cross rivers that did rage. McClellan's attention turned to a neck of land some seventy miles south-east of Richmond, where the Unionists occupied the fort of Monroe. This area is known as the Peninsula, and measures fifty miles in length and fifteen miles in breadth. The terrain is hostile to say the least, with numerous woods and streams; no wonder so few people dwell in such a place. The ground is mainly low-lying sand and is flat, with few vantage points for observation or cannon.

It has been reported in the newspapers that McClellan arrived at Fort Monroe on 2nd April. He had reputedly amassed a giant force: 121,500 troops; 14,592 animals; 1,150 wagons; forty-four batteries of artillery and seventy-four ambulances, the logistics of which are staggering and which it is claimed, took 400 vessels three weeks to transport from Washington along the Potomac into the bay of Chesapeake. This Goliath became lighter by 20,000 troops who were transferred to other duties, but nevertheless remained a formidable force to be reckoned with. Richmond seemed oblivious to the threat. Thankfully McClellan is a cautious man.

The Confederate commander of Yorktown, Major General Magruder, had problems of his own: the Confederate navy was unable to bombard the Union positions in front of Yorktown. Strangely enough, the Confederates are now making use of the Yorktown fortifications built by the British. However the fortifications across from Yorktown at Glouster Point are of recent construction.

Magruder desired knowledge of the enemy, both in its strength and disposition, and employed a most unusual implement for this purpose: a balloon. A man was hoisted aloft under the balloon in a basket, and the balloon was hauled down when the task was complete. McClellan is a man who shows concern for his troops, abhorring unnecessary loss of life, be it that of friend or foe. I suspect he does favour siege to assault. Magruder is on the other hand a colourful individual, given to deception. One of his ploys was to exaggerate the strength of his command by having his troops march several times over, in sight of the enemy.

The Union offensive did start on 4th April with an advance on Yorktown by one force of corps strength, commanded by Brigadier General Heintzelman. A second corps, commanded by Brigadier Keyes, was to seize an area four miles north of Yorktown, thus flanking the place, while a third corps, commanded by Brigadier General Sumner, was ready to support either of the other two.

On 5th April the weather turned foul, thus delaying the advance. One force waited in front of Yorktown. The second force did encounter the River Warwick, not shown on the maps.

Keyes did cross the dam at Lee's Mill with a small force, but when the Confederates brought up reinforcements, the Union troops withdrew. The Confederate defence line had come close to being breached. Here was a case of a greater Confederate force not advancing and thus obliging the enemy. It has been rumoured that McClellan believed he had 100,000 Confederates facing him across the Warwick, thanks to one of Magruder's deceptions. In fact only 11,000 faced the Union corps. A similar thought, that Yorktown was being reinforced, was also in McClellans mind.

On the 16th, Smith with a sizeable force did cross the Warwick at the Burnt Chimney dam. Reinforced, the Confederates regained the dam. Thus a second opportunity had been lost by the Union. By now Richmond had finally acknowledged the threat, and Johnston started to move his army from north of Richmond. The force was now above 50,000, thus the Union advantage of numbers had fallen from eleven to one, to two to one.

Yorktown was now under siege. The Union preparations included hauling ten-ton cannons into position behind earth parapets. These monsters can lob a shell weighing 200 pounds. Could the gallant town withstand such weapons? It has been claimed that 114 such monsters faced the town, plus 300 various cannons.

No further news has been forthcoming from this area, however, several days ago I did learn of other happenings. In the Shenandoah, Jackson moved slowly, enticing Banks to follow, resulting in a brief clash near Strasburg on 2nd April. Johnston now wished the valley force to disrupt the flow of Union material from the valley to McClellan, and for this purpose he did instruct General Ewell with his 8,500 force near Brandy Station to work with Jackson. The Confederate forces did march most of April to confuse Banks.

The other information came from further west. Major General Van Dorn did venture forth from Arkansas with his 16,000 troops and did battle with a Union force of 11,000, commanded by Brigadier General Curtis. Van Dorn was pushed back to the Arkansas River. The taking of Nashville did stir the Confederate states, who sent men and arms to Johnston. In early April he had amassed 40,000 at Corinth, including 10,000 from Pensacola commanded by Major General Braxton, and 5,000 from New Orleans, commanded by Brigadier General Ruggles. Polk in the meantime had taken 5,000 to reinforce Island Ten, in the Mississippi River near New Madrid.

Now as to the Union in the area. Grant had transported and landed his army at Pittsburg Landing, just twenty-two miles from Corinth. There he stayed on the orders of Halleck, the overall commander, until Buell did march his 55,000 army from Nashville over a distance of 122 miles to the small town of Savannah in Tennessee, just nine miles from Grant. Buell's march was greatly delayed by the Confederates destroying bridges. Sherman was second-in-command to Grant's force and had deployed his troops in a line four miles inland. Many of the troops had only recently joined. Neither Grant nor Sherman expected an attack, thus few defences were prepared.

Johnston and Beauregard had a force equal to that of Grant's, and needed to destroy Grant's force before Buell was able to advance. Beauregard being an excellent organiser, he was left to form the four corps, the commanders of which were Major General Breckinridge, Major General Polk, Major General Hardee and Major General Bragg.

Time for the race to reach Grant. Who would be the first – Johnston or Buell? Beauregard planned to march on 3rd April, and to attack on the following day with Hardee in the lead, but was delayed so the march didn't commence until a day later. He was finally in position on the 5th. Bragg formed his troops behind Hardee, but his left flank was missing one regiment which had got lost. It was now noon, and by the time the lost regiment did arrive it was night so the attack had to be postponed until next day, Sunday 6th. Rain, mud and congestion on the few tracks were the prime factors.

Now a remarkable event, which I can only consider as luck, took place. Some inexperienced Confederates fired their muskets to check that they were still functioning after the rain, thus making a great din. Then it was discovered that a Union drummer had been making a similar noise on his drum. Neither of these incidents aroused the Union army who slumbered on, innocent of the fact that just beyond their lines was a strong Confederate force.

Equally as puzzling was the fact that many units of the Union force had encountered Confederate forces as early as 4th April, yet when this was reported to Sherman he simply disregarded it and took no further action. Truly I consider that fortune was indeed smiling on Johnston, for had the Union commander taken notice then he might have caught the Confederate force in disarray and thus inflicted a serious defeat.

Yet another strange incident occurred which, it is claimed, triggered the battle. At 3 a.m. Sunday morning, 300 Union troops were sent to conduct a reconnaissance near the little church of Shiloh and exchanged fire with the Confederates. On the Union side Lieutenant Klinger was the first to be shot to death and now there was no escape – no chance of a withdrawal by either side. The Confederates advanced, driving back the reinforcements sent forward by the Union. I understand that there was another strange and inexplicable decision by Johnston who went to the front lines to direct matters, leaving Beauregard to organize and direct men and supplies. I understand this to mean that the officer in this position actually controls the battle. Added to this was the fact that neither could agree on a unified plan. Johnston's plan had Polk to the left, Bragg in the centre, and Hardee to the right, with Breckinridge in reserve in order to cut off the Union from the river, and start an encircling movement to trap the army thereby forcing them to surrender. Beauregard's plan was simply to attack in three waves and drive the Union force eastward into Tennessee.

Although Sherman had been informed of the situation, he still could not believe it, and went to see for himself. Prior to his arrival the Confederates had charged a Union camp, surprising those therein, who ran to the rear. They came to a halt on a ridge and prepared to meet the hordes of grey. Sherman arrived and was nearly shot dead; the man alongside him was instantly killed.

Finally Sherman acted. In some sections the Union regiments were routed, while elsewhere they fought hard to hold their positions. The Confederates were not succeeding with their objectives. Grant arrived on the battlefield around 9 a.m.; Buell's regiments had also started to arrive that morning. Johnston seemed to have lost his chance and the race: an attack on the 4th or even the 5th might well have spelt disaster for Grant. However, for the moment the Union line broke and a retreat for the river and the boats ensued. By 10 a.m. the Union left wing had gone, and both flanks were being turned. Sherman ordered a withdrawal. The fighting had been continuous for seven hours and had been both heavy and bloody. Many Union soldiers had savage wounds. I feel sickened that I cannot find the will to write here the descriptions given in the newspapers.

While the Confederates paused to eat the food they had captured, the Union force was able to form a new line. In the meantime the Confederate forces were drifting about and the grand assaults had diminished to small, scattered ones. Whilst Johnston was preparing to relaunch a mass attack confusion arose; at this point both sides opened up with a bombardment. There followed several charges by the Confederates on two of the Union positions: namely the Hornets Nest and the Sunken Road. Terrible losses and injuries were sustained by the attackers. Charge after charge was made against the Hornets Nest and the Sunken Road, but to no avail. Many of those wounded in the fields were burnt to death when cannon did ignite the undergrowth. The battle still had not abated at 2.30 p.m. The Confederate command seemed uncoordinated: the corps commanders were acting on their own, whilst Beauregard was sending troops to where the battle sounded the loudest.

I am told by some military persons that it is not considered good policy to attack a stronghold without the employment of twice the force of the defenders. The Hornets Nest might well have succumbed quickly had the 17,000 Confederates attacked en bloc against the 5,000 defenders; to send in less than 4,000 at a time was suicidal. Sadly while Johnston led his forces in an attack near the Sunken Road, he was wounded and shortly afterwards bled to death.

Beauregard assumed command and immediately made a blunder. Instead of driving back the weak sections adjacent to the Hornets Nest, he determined to destroy this strong point. After some thirteen charges, it was decided to change tactics; sixty-two cannons were assembled, and opened fire at 4.30 p.m. The area became the valley of death for the Union defenders. Johnston's plan seemed about to happen by accident rather than design: the line either side of the strongpoint did start to bend back in the form of a horseshoe. Ammunition was also dangerously low and then the run to the boats started. The Confederates pursued, firing all the time. The toll was mounting for the Union troops.

Finally the Hornets Nest surrendered at 5.30 p.m.; various trapped units of Union troops surrendered elsewhere. Some Union regiments conducted an orderly fighting rearguard withdrawal, others simply ran. Grant had by now formed a new three-mile line near Pittsburg Landing. Fresh troops were arriving and preparations were underway to prepare for the sector where the Confederate main attack was expected.

After twelve hours of fighting the Confederates were rested and fed. Their last meal had been the day before; now there were plentiful supplies of Union stores. They had also to gather in the prisoners; thus quietness settled over the area. Buell had by now arrived with his 35,000 troops; the Confederates would face a strong Union line the next day. However, the Confederate commanders did try one further attack. All came to grief; they were also without ammunition and finally the fighting stopped. Now the moans and groans, the screams of injured soldiers, Union and Confederate, filled the night air. Neither command had any organized means of attending to them. The whole scene became a bizarre sight with heavy, cold rain and flashes of lightning. I imagine many a soldier that night might well have wondered whether he had descended into Dante's Inferno. Added to this two Union gunboats kept up a bombardment although they did little damage from such a distance.

Early next morning Grant advanced with his 40,000, mainly fresh, troops against 20,000 tired and hungry Confederates. Nevertheless the soldiers did fight tenaciously until 3.30 p.m. when they started to withdraw in an orderly fashion. Colonel Jordon with 2,000 troops did fight a rearguard action then withdrew. Fortunately the hard fighting prevented pursuit by the Union army. The Confederate army had not marched far before dropping with exhaustion.

The following day the Confederates started their march to Corinth, leaving 350 cavalry to keep watch against pursuit. Sherman did in fact advance with some 2,000 troops to check that the Confederates had left the area; he had no intention of being surprised again. Forrest did charge the Union force with his cavalry, forcing a halt. The final shot of the battle came when Forrest was wounded while in the midst of the Union soldiers.

Shiloh has been the first battle to have involved about thirty hours of fighting, all which can be described as fierce. It was by far the bloodiest contest to date: 1,700 dead and 8,000 wounded on each side. The figures indicate that the Confederates did lose more of their small force than the larger Union army which included Buell's force.

In Corinth the Confederates faced another enemy which was taking its toll. Few medicines were available: eight out of ten men died after amputation, and dysentery was rife.

I did mention some of Polk's force had been transferred to Island Ten. News has arrived that the Union force did attack the Island in early March with little success. The Confederates had 7,000 troops, nineteen cannon and five batteries on the river bank, plus a floating battery and a flotilla of gunboats. They were able to keep at bay some 20,000 troops commanded by Major General Pope. Flag Officer Foote did command six gunboats and eleven mortar boats. The Union force did show enterprise by constructing a fifty-foot-wide channel to bypass the island which took six hundred men three weeks to complete.

A Union gunboat did slip by the island and on 6th April did destroy many of the land-based batteries. The next day, with the aid of a second gunboat, the Union troops landed on the island. Most of the Confederates were able to withdraw; the rest surrendered so that the island was in Union hands by 9 p.m. Those who had withdrawn were captured near Tiptonville. This was indeed a serious blow: three generals and 5,000 troops were prisoners of the Union.

News has arrived that Major General Halleck has taken command of the Union forces at Pittsburg Landing. He is assembling a force expected to comprise 100,000 men and 200 cannon. It is rumoured that Corinth is his objective.

The newspapers on both sides are very critical of Grant being taken by surprise and of Beauregard for bad planning. It is reported that Van Dorn's force has linked up with Beauregard's at Corinth, thus making a total of about 50,000 men.

Yesterday the newspapers did report that Halleck's army is on the march but are only managing to cover one mile a day; the distance to Corinth is twenty-two miles.

I regret to have to write and inform you of a further setback for the Confederates. The fort of Macon was heavily bombarded on 25th April and did surrender to the Union forces and warships after ten hours. In the Gulf of Mexico the Union was assembling a force on Ship Island, near the estuary of the Mississippi. This was indeed a formidable force consisting of twenty-two ships plus several others that Rear Admiral Farragut had brought with him, making a total of 192 guns. Commander Porter had assembled a mortar flotilla. In the meantime General Butler arrived with 18,000 troops.

The navy's first task was to gain access to the river itself. At the head of the river are fingers of land forming five channels.

The mortar boats selected one channel which suited their shallow keels; the seagoing warships had problems, but finally force a way through so that the navy was in the Mississippi on 8th April. Major General Lovall had declared martial law in late March when the true intent was learned. The 168,000 populace was now disturbed. The Spanish citadel of St Philip is a mighty stronghold, as is also the fort of Jackson, which is very much of a modern construction. The forts' commander, Brigadier General Duncan, did form a barrier across the river within range of his guns, thus any assault by land would face a whole network of fortifications stretching across four miles.

In Jefferson City, north of New Orleans, two ironclads that were swift and strong were under construction; many considered them invincible and expected them to make short work of the Union fleet, thus freeing New Orleans of the inconvenient blockade. These vessels were then to sail north, to dispose of the Union river fleet in the northern Mississippi. Meanwhile a Confederate fleet of rams, tugs and steamers was being prepared to meet the enemy should they approach New Orleans by river.

The Union mortar boats opened fire at 9 a.m. on 18th April, their target Fort Jackson. By dusk 1,000 shells had been lobbed at the fort and for three days this continued. On the night of Easter Day the Union was able to open the river barrier, yet apart from the continuing bombardment nothing changed by the 23rd April. The attempt to run the gauntlet commenced at 2 a.m. on the 24th. In the meantime the Confederate fleet had arrived but, being outgunned, could do little apart from minor damage to a number of the enemy and sink one warship. By midday the Union fleet was sailing unopposed towards New Orleans.

Wisely, Lovall decided it best to withdraw in order to save lives, since the Union warships were certain to fire on the city. The populace did riot in anger and frustration and many cotton bales and other goods were set alight. At 1 p.m. on the 25th, the fleet arrived and two officers went ashore amid a hostile crowd: Mayor Monroe could not surrender as the city was under martial law; Lovall refused to surrender but lifted the martial law before departing to rejoin his force which was withdrawing. Monroe and Farragut continued the discussions the following day and the outcome was finally settled when Duncan surrendered the two forts on the 28th. When he arrived in the city on the following day and informed Mayor Monroe of this, that saw an end of it. The notorious Major General Butler had landed his troops, and quickly occupied the two forts prior to entering the city.

Thus, sir, I end this sorrowful account of mishaps for the Confederacy. Yet with the vastness of the land I do not believe that the Union has sufficient men to occupy and hold all the land.

The Union intent now seems clearer: namely, to use the Mississippi as a wedge to divide the Confederacy in two, and to force a surrender by occupying ports, many of which are now in Union hands. Their attempt to seize Richmond seems pointless since they would not damage the morale of the people, or break their resolve. Occupying Richmond will not stop the Confederate government: the place is not of importance; while the government continues to exist, so the Confederacy exists.

Sir, although things appear bad they are by no means desperate. How can the whole might of the Union prevent a Confederate government?

Time is the most valuable asset the Confederacy has.

Sir, I am, and remain, your obedient servant. . .

Richmond
30 May 1862

Sir,

The campaigns mentioned in my letter of April are continuing. In the Peninsula there has been news about Yorktown, Williamsburg, West Point, Norfolk, Hanover and Drewry's Bluff. Each day that passes indicates the Union intentions towards Richmond.

In Shenandoah there is news about McDowell, Front Royal and Winchester, and in Tennessee, Baton Rouge and Corinth.

McClellan's technique had worked for him at Yorktown, the mixture of intimidation and siege helping him to capture the town without loss. Johnston was sensible enough to realize that little was to be gained from the defence and so by stealth he withdrew his entire force under cover of darkness. The Union announced the capture on 4th May. It came as a surprise and relief to the Union army. That Sunday afternoon Union cavalry did engage the Confederates outside Williamsburg. Magruder had built a second line of defence before the town, with Fort Magruder as the central large bastion, plus thirteen other redoubts. The line extended four miles, its flanks impassable with creeks and marshes. Rifle pits were scattered over a plain, and the approach roads were strewn with debris.

On the morning of 5th May and in heavy rain, Smith's division was in front of the fort. Sumner was in command of the assumed pursuit. In the meantime a division commanded by Hooker arrived and commenced an attack at 7.30 a.m. with cannon. Many of the crew fled when they received their first taste of battle, and another battery had to give assistance. The Confederates did reinforce the sector and pushed back the Union forces while other Union forces seemed to be idle. At 4 p.m. a Union force came up and was able to push the Confederates back to the fort. In the meantime Sumner had sent a force to occupy two empty redoubts at the north end of the line. The Confederates realized the situation and did charge, mistakenly thinking that they had routed the enemy, but the Union force had been lying low until the last moment, and when the attackers were close they did open fire with deadly results, following on with a bayonet charge. In the space of twenty-three minutes the battle had been won by the Union.

Next morning the Confederates continued their withdrawal as planned. The losses were 1,603 Confederates dead, missing and wounded. Union losses were 2,239 including 456 dead. Was this a worthwhile price to pay with Richmond only fifty miles away?

I understand that at this point President Lincoln joined in the campaign when he arrived at Fort Monroe, and directed an attack on Norfolk, the base for the Confederate warship *Virginia*, capturing it without a fight on 10th May. At 4.58 a.m. next morning the *Virginia* blew up.

McClellan had captured West Point on 7th May and his advance seemed to be going well despite the many setbacks.

Meanwhile here in Richmond there was panic with much talk of razing the capital to the ground. General Lee was the only man who remained calm; he had seen that the immediate threat came from five Union gunboats, just one day away on the River James. The General improved some fortifications eight miles to the south of the capital at Drewry's Bluff and by the 15th, they were ready for the Union ships. After three and a hours of pommelling by the defenders, the enemy ships did retreat, licking their wounds.

By 24th May, McClellan had his troops in position near Richmond. Some of the citizens did claim they could see Union soldiers although I don't know how true this was. The army command did confirm for me that Union troops formed a line from Mechanicsville, six miles north-east of Richmond, to Seven Pines, six miles to the east of the capital. It was expected that a second Union army, commanded by McDowell, would advance from the north near Fredericksburg, midway between Washington and Richmond.

Washington was extremely concerned that both Johnston and Jackson were a threat, proving that Jackson's scheme was succeeding, so the President diverted many of McDowell's force to deal with Jackson.

Jackson must have been pleased that his small force was hoodwinking the Union to the extent that they were now arraying against him with the three armies of McDowell, Banks and Fremont.

Ashby's cavalry did cause Banks to slow his advance, first near Strasburg, and again at Stoney Creek. It was here that Banks waited for two weeks. It was now 16th April and Jackson's force was waiting ten miles away at Mount Jackson. On that day Banks made a move across Stoney Creek, and came upon Jackson, who again caused Banks some problems. Then his force moved back to Harrisonburg on the 18th. Banks and Jackson each sent a small force to Luray Valley: Ashby to destroy bridges, and the Union to secure them.

Jackson seemed to disappear after that, leaving Banks to think he had left the Valley, with the result that Banks slowly moved his force to Harrisonburg, and then sent messages requesting to join McClellan or McDowell for the attack on Richmond.

Information I received from Washington indicates that Jackson's activities, or lack of them, are causing considerable concern, with some even going so far as to state that Jackson could suddenly attack the capital. Because of this, many troops were held back to defend Washington and only part of Banks' force was instructed to join McDowell.

Jackson, in the meantime, was making changes among his commanders after several had behaved poorly in recent conflicts. He also had reappeared at the end of April near Staunton, and was in contact with a Union force and, in the early part of this month, was on the move again. With an elaborate series of marches, which it is said confused his own men as well as the Union, he reached McDowell in the Allegheny Mountains, to the west side of the Valley, a long way south, and there achieved his objective: to confront Milroy's 6,000 troops with his superior 10,000. The Union commander had no choice but to fight or be cut to pieces by cannon if he attempted a withdrawal. He decided to attack, and so at 4.30 p.m. on 8th May he did charge the enemy position. The fight ended around 9 p.m. when darkness fell. The Confederate losses were 498 and the Union 256. Jackson's men had marched 200 miles in just eighteen days.

In the meantime General Shield's force of 11,000 was marching to link up with McDowell at Fredericksburg, thus leaving Banks with 7,600 men who were somewhat scattered. One group of 1,000 guarding Front Royal was isolated by Jackson from Banks at Strasburg, by destroying a depot between Strasburg and Front Royal, on the 23rd. By 2 p.m. the battle started and soon the Union force was driven out of the town to a nearby hill, running amok when they realized their escape route was about to be blocked. Jackson and Ewell's troops were hindered in the pursuit, but the cavalry was available and caught up with the enemy, charging them several times. The Union side lost 904 men, 750 of whom were taken prisoner.

That night a small force of Confederate cavalry did come close to Strasburg from the south, lulling Banks into believing that was where the attack would come. Finally his staff convinced him to withdraw to Winchester, and the next day the Union force was on the move. A story was told how a regiment of Confederate Marylanders did battle with a regiment of Union Marylanders, the Confederates winning the day.

Jackson and Ewell now set off in pursuit of Banks. The Union rearguard had to fight constantly, and at one stage the Confederate cannon was able to pound the rear of the retreating Union column. Elsewhere, Confederate cavalry made a surprise attack at Newtown. Sunday 25th May saw Jackson together with Ewell at Winchester. The Confederates did strongly charge all the hills where the Union troops were entrenched and it wasn't long before the Union force was routed, and fled all the way back across the Potomac. Jackson had succeeded in his plans: Banks had lost 3,500 men – 35 per cent of his command – and been driven out of Virginia.

An acquaintance of mine, recently returned from Washington, did tell me that the President and Union command are gravely concerned that the capital is now under threat. Thus McDowell, who was poised to march and join McClellan at Richmond, once Shield's troops had arrive from the Valley, now found himself halted once more. It would seem that Jackson had convinced the Union that the Confederate army was strong, ready to cross the Potomac and march on Washington. McClellan was on his own in hostile land without hope of further help.

I also have to report that on the borders of Tennessee and Mississippi the railway junction of Corinth was taken by Halleck. The Union cannon did open fire on 29th May. Beauregard could not defend such a place, but created one of his renowned deceptions, giving Halleck the impression that he faced a greatly reinforced enemy. Thus while the Union hesitated, the Confederates were able to slip away without inviting pursuit. In the meantime the river community of Baton Rouge, in the State of Louisiana, was occupied by the Union after the navy had sailed upriver from its victory at New Orleans.

There is one further matter to report, which refers to the situation near Richmond. There was a brief encounter on 27th May between a Union division advancing from McClellan, whose north wing was extending a line to Hanover Court House to be nearer McDowell's army, when they encountered a Confederate brigade. The Confederates did charge and overcame the first line of the Union position, which was finally recovered by Union reinforcements. The Union side brought up further troops and did countercharge, leaving the Confederates no choice but to withdraw. 200 men were dead or wounded and 500 taken prisoner. The Union losses were 355.

More alarming news: McDowell is reported to have been seen a mere twenty-five miles north of Hanover Court House. Then relief came on the 28th when it was learned that McDowell's army had turned round and was marching back to Fredericksburg. I did say a prayer for Jackson, who I feel sure was responsible for causing this action by the Union forces. Methinks Washington is more concerned lest it be lost to the Confederates, as this might well mean the disintegration of those states at present in the Union, and a shift to the Confederacy by those non-committed states that are wavering.

Secessionists lurk everywhere in the Union states and it takes only a small incident to provoke major discontent. Dissatisfaction with the administrative conduct of the so-called war and neglect of domestic matters are subjects ripe for mischief-making.

Sir, I am, and remain, your obedient servant. . .

Richmond
15 July 1862

Sir,

I have elected to remain here until the present crisis is resolved one way or the other. In the meantime, I have requested our representative in New York to ascertain the opinion of the business community regarding the two possible situations: firstly, the effects should Washington fall, and secondly, the effects should this present conflict of arms continue through another year, bearing in mind the activities of the belligerent naval forces along the whole of the coastline from New Jersey to Virginia.

I visited a military acquaintance to learn the happenings, and of Johnston's intentions and his plan to deal with the presence of the enemy force. An attack had been set for 29th May, the objective to strike McClellan's divided forces near Mechanicsville. This was immediately cancelled when news of McDowell's return to Fredericksburg was received. A reconnaissance was carried out on the 13th to view the disposition of McClellan's left wing which it was confirmed was in disarray.

The Union defence in the area comprised of Brigadier General Casey's division, just west of Seven Pines. This was a strong position extending south to White Oak Swamp. To his rear were the divisions of Couch and Kearney, between Seven Pines and a place known as Bottom's Bridge. To the south of them was Hooker's division. However, the northern sector of this wing was found to be weak in the region of the railway station at Fair Oaks. In this area are marshes extending as far as the Chickahominy River. On the far bank Sumner's 17,000-strong corps was encamped.

The plan of battle, set for the next day, was for a left wing commanded by Smith to hold Magruder, and A. P. Hill's divisions on the upper Chickahominy to watch for the two Union corps in the area. Whiting's division would support the right wing command of Longstreet. The right wing comprised three divisions, some 40,000 troops. This force was divided into three: Huger to lead his force south-east then north to Seven Pines; D. H. Hill's force to approach Seven Pines from the east, while Longstreet's force would join with Whiting and attack from the north towards the Fair Oaks station.

Providence seemed to smile on Johnston, as the night before there came rain from the heavens that did swamp bridges and turned the Chickahominy into a raging torrent thus isolating the Union forces at Seven Pines and Fair Oaks.

That morning the citizens sensed something was afoot and did congregate on a hill to the east of the capital: would this day's activities seal the fate of their city one way or the other? Strangely, as I have remarked throughout the past two months, few did leave, which surely shows confidence in the commanders of the army. In such adversity and against a greater host they were confident they would win with Johnston, their greatest general.

Eventually, after a four-hour delay, D. H. Hill did attack at 1 p.m. and soon broke through the earthworks, forcing a retreat as far back as Seven Pines, where Union troops reformed, reinforced by two of Keyes's regiments. These two regiments did counter-attack and regained some lost ground. The Confederates did retreat only as far as the enemy redoubt, taken a few hours earlier.

In the meantime a second Confederate regiment split the Union line between Seven Pines and White Oak, then turned south to flank the Union force at Seven Pines. The northern force of Longstreet and Whiting occupied Fair Oaks, then came under attack, and after three charges, the Confederates came close to the Union cannon and their defences. However, at that moment Sumner arrived to support the hard-pressed Union line.

It seemed now to have become a stalemate, and at 7 p.m. Johnston arrived at the battlefield, whereupon he was wounded. At the same moment President Davis and General Lee did arrive. Command went to Smith. The gentleman took stock: at Fair Oaks, it was impasse; at Seven Pines, they had managed to push Union troops beck to their third defensive line, a mile east of Seven Pines; the Union was bringing up reinforcements and to make matters worse, the weather was wet and cold that night. Smith did dither and seemingly had no plans either to withdraw, defend or attack; each option worried him.

Longstreet and Hill elected to determine the enemy's disposition the next morning; thus at 6.30 a.m. the Confederates did advance at one point to engage a Union force. Hooker was directly east of Seven Pines; next to him to the northwest was Kearny, and west of him was Richardson, whose right wing was at Fair Oaks. At right angles to him along a north-east line was Sedwick. Opposing Sedwick was Whiting's force, whilst D. H. Hill did face Richardson, Kearny and Hooker.

By 2 p.m. the battle was over, with no one the victor. There had been a series of blunders on the Confederate side owing to bad planning, inappropriate orders and lack of knowledge of the terrain. In the middle, the three Confederate forces had been unaware of each other and therefore attacked independently, thus enabling the Union defenders to enter the gaps between them and flank the respective forces, causing considerable losses and forcing a retreat. To the south, the Confederates were more successful against Hooker's forces. Once again confusion over identity did enable a Confederate force to surprise and defeat a Union force.

Elsewhere, Confederate commanders were repeating the mistakes of previous battles by not committing their whole force in a single attack against the defended position. This did demonstrate to me, a mere novice in military matters, the futility of sending a small attack force against a stronger defending force. To repeat the exercise several times over is sheer folly and results in a tragic, needless loss of life.

This was by far the biggest and bloodiest fight to date, the Confederates losing 6,134 of which 980 were killed, while the Union losses amounted to 5,031, including 790 dead. This swampland did nothing to change the situation, yet produced two dramatic events. The battle made McClellan much more cautious, and he elected for a siege at Seven Pines and Fair Oaks, which areas were now fortified. The other event was the appointment of Robert E. Lee as Field Commander in the east.

Meanwhile in western Virginia, Jackson was still causing problems for the three Union forces of Banks, Fremont and Shields. Jackson needed to protect Strasburg until all his forces and wagons, plus prisoners, had passed through heading south. On 1st June Ewell did position himself west of the town to hold off any advance by Fremont. Only the Stonewall brigade was awaited; then Jackson's entire army would have escaped President Lincoln's trap. The brigade set out from Harper's Ferry in the afternoon of 31st May, trudging through rain, travelling through Winchester to arrive at Newtown at 10 p.m. having marched thirty-five miles. The next day they arrived at Strasburg and rested a while, then the whole of Jackson's army moved south. The Union trap had failed, although Jackson was not out of danger as both Shields and Fremont were not far away.

Ashby's cavalry prevented Fremont's forces from advancing with speed but Ashby was attacked just south of Harrisonburg on 6th June, by Union cavalry which he forced to retreat. When the Union troops reformed, Ashby attacked again and was shot to death. The Confederates did cause the Union defenders to retreat. Finally Jackson prepared to face Shields and Fremont, having prepared good positions overlooking Port Republic, whilst Ewell had a strong defence on a ridge, seven miles south-east of Harrisonburg, near the village of Cross Keys.

On 8th June Union cavalry entered Port Republic but were driven out: the Union officers made the mistake of trying to hold the bridge instead of burning it, which gave Jackson, an escape route. He might otherwise have been trapped between two Union forces. The same day at Cross Keys, Fremont had sent five of his twenty-four regiments to attack Ewell. They were slaughtered. Brigadier General Trimble did well in this fight, putting a swift end to the Union attack before mounting a charge. For the rest of the day he remained in an advanced position of his defences, but suffered no further attack by the Union force. Thus ended this brief fight, leaving Fremont with a loss of 684 men, while Ewell had lost 288.

On the misty morning of 9th June Jackson, without having carried out a reconnaissance, did order the Stonewall brigade to charge and forced the men straight into a trap. Union cannons on high ground did fire down on the Confederate brigade and, with furious fire to their front, the brigade was caught, unable to move. Three times the Confederates struggled to the top of the high ground to charge the cannons, then, just when all seemed lost, a fresh force of Union troops having arrived on the high ground, another Confederate force emerged. The Union went into retreat leaving the Confederates to turn the cannon on the Union troops below. Ewell arrived in time to fall on the flank of the Union line; other Confederate forces were arriving, and thus the Union side had slowly to give way.

It was indeed a hard-fought battle by both sides. Jackson suffered a loss of 615, his greatest since the campaign started, whilst the Union lost 1,018 men including 615 taken prisoner. This did truly show that a small force could easily distract the enemy, forcing him to revise his plans.

I understand that Fremont withdrew to Mount Jackson, Shields to Luray, and Jackson, having first been to Brown's Gap in the Blue Ridge, and facing no further attack by Union forces, established his headquarters near Weyer's Cave.

This also confirmed for me how it is possible for a large body of men and wagons, plus equipment, to roam and not be detected.

Some brief naval battles took place north end of the River Mississippi when Union ships sailing down the river near Fort Pillow were intercepted on 10th May and severely damaged. On 6th June the Union fleet returned, this time reinforced, and did damage or destroy all but one of the eight Confederate crafts near Memphis. Fort Pillow was evacuated by the Confederates on 4th June and the Mayor of Memphis did surrender the town soon after the battle two days later. Union ships from New Orleans did arrive near Vicksburg, expecting the town to surrender, but were snubbed. Farragut decided that it would not be possible to attack from land or sea and thus withdrew.

The Company representative in New York sent me newspapers bragging that Charleston would soon be punished as the prime evil-doer for its leading role as midwife in assisting the birth of the Confederacy. Charleston, I am informed, is heavily fortified, its defences being increased all the time. The Union will not find this city timid in defence and, should it dare to have the effrontery to trespass in the city's waters, will pay dearly for it.

The Union force is said to be gathering at Stone Inlet; if this is so then the objective will be James Island.

I have no further information to date.

Sir, I am, and remain, your obedient servant. . .

Richmond
30 June 1862

Sir,

I have to report that progress is slow for the proposed expedition by our New York representative. If unresolved I plan to visit the offices and discuss the matter and will advise you accordingly.

Regarding my conflict report (I cannot yet bring myself to accept this as war), you will find limited news. The Union did have the audacity to attempt an attack on Charleston. Brigadier General Benham did land and attack James Island, on 16th June, which advance suffered many losses, partly as a result of being shelled by their own ships. Some reached the defences. Another Union division was preparing to attack and might well have overwhelmed the small garrison when Benham did order a withdrawal. Thus ended the attempt. The Union force did suffer a loss of 683 and rumour has it that Benham is under arrest. Near Vicksburg, the Union ships did once more approach on 25th June and engaged the shore batteries for two days without success. On 28th they ran the gauntlet with eleven ships, three of which retreated while the others managed to pass without much damage. The townspeople did have a rude and frightful awakening that morning when some of the shells fell on the city by accident.

With Lee now in command, an army of 50,000 still face a Union army of 100,000. McClellan is busy building bridges in this rain and seems to have become extra cautious since the incident at Seven Pines. Richmond celebrated the daring exploits of Jeb Stuart who led a force 1,200 horsemen out around the north flank of McClellan's army, inflicting damage on the way. He rode past the rear of the enemy, passing the southern flank, and returned to Richmond on 15th June, which feat took just three days to accomplish and greatly cheered the people and the army.

On 26th June McClellan did advance his line west from Seven Pines. The fighting around Oak Grove lasted for only three hours until the Union force stopped for a reason as yet unknown. The Union had gained half a mile of ground and suffered a loss of 626 men, while the Confederates lost 441.

Jackson, I understand, did march 120 miles from the Valley, setting out on 16th June with a force of 18,500, plus extra divisions and a brigade. On 26th Magruder did once again demonstrate with his small force, quelling any action by McClellan. Meanwhile in the north, Jackson intended to attack at dawn but was delayed. The battle started at 3 p.m. when Hill did attack Mechanicsville, driving back the Union defenders. However, the Confederates were prevented from advancing by strong fortifications and lost many men. Jackson had indeed arrived by 5 p.m but his force was so tired that the men rested all night and thus did not outflank the Union lines as planned. The fighting ended at 9 p.m. with little result other than the loss of 1,484 men. During the night the Union troops withdrew to prepare new defences at Gains Mill.

Lee made a three-pronged attack against the line on the 27th, and throughout the day more and more regiments of the Confederate force joined the battle; there were many charges and counter-charges. By 7 p.m. the Confederates were attacking along the whole Union line, soon forcing the Union troops to withdraw, being 56,000 in number against 35,000 Union troops. The Union forces received few reinforcements from McClellan, the remaining 60,000 being mesmerised by Magruder's grand show of deception. The Confederates were well pleased: two Union regiments captured and fourteen cannon. This might have been a rout had the attackers not been exhausted. The day's fighting resulted in 8,751 Confederate losses as opposed to 6,837 on the Union side, including 2,836 prisoners.

On the 29th the Confederates did once more break the Union line at Savage Station, and later near White Oak. The Union troops in front of Magruder now started to withdraw, the entire Union army retreating from Richmond. Again there was confusion at Savage Station; Jackson did not appear in support of Magruder and no one seem to be in command of the Union forces. The Confederates were halted and at dusk the Union troops withdrew.

On the 30th there was a bloody and determined battle at Glendale where Jackson and Huger could have achieved great things, but strangely stayed idle, only Longstreet and Hill attempting to force the issue. Neither side was victorious come nightfall. Confederate losses: 3,300; Union 2,853 including 1,130 taken prisoner. I did hear that President Davis and other officials visited the battlefield: a most foolhardy act in view of the shelling close by. The Confederates showed enterprise by driving forward an engine with a cannon mounted on it, protected by armour plating. Sadly the crude device did not prove itself.

That, sir, concludes the activity to date. Should Lee drive McClellan off Confederate soil, perhaps President Lincoln may have a change of heart.

Sir, I am, and remain, your obedient servant. . .

Nine
Lee's advancement

Richmond
30 July 1862

Sir,

Next month I shall be in New York, to discuss various options to enable the company's progression and to examine the business situation there. It is important now to consider this factor and future projects in the light of this protracted conflict; heaven forbid this should continue for years.

In my last letter I did write regarding the battle around Richmond which reached a bloody, gory climax the following day, 1st July. McClellan still commanded a large part of the original 100,000, most of which was concentrated on Malvern Hill with a host of cannon, originally those intended for siege. Lee's battle-line formed a mile-long crescent: Whiting with three brigades was on the left; D. H. Hill in the centre with five brigades, and Huger and Magruder on the right with eight brigades. On the left in reserve were Ewell's and Jackson's divisions; on the right in reserve were the divisions of A. P. Hill and Longstreet. It took time to bring all units into position and, as usual, the unfamiliar terrain caused many delays. The main flaw seems to have been that Lee did not have a plan, as had been the case on the preceding days of this fight. and this. together with being unable to bring artillery into effective positions. combined to reduce the chances of destroying McClellan's army.

Malvern Hill is situated near the River James, thus providing the Union with the additional support of the gunboats. Had the Confederates been able to concentrate the cannon on a nearby high ground they could have engaged the enemy cannon, allowing the infantry to attack without being cut to pieces by the long-range cannon fire, but this was impossible as the cannon were still clogged in the rear, although some divisions did have a few of their own. The units on the right were in the best position to observe the effects of the duel and so, at the favourable moment, they would give a yell and attack whereupon the other commanders would follow suit. At 4 p.m. with still no move forward two messages were handed to Lee from his left, one assuming that Union movement indicated a withdrawal while the second message assumed that some units had advanced successfully. The left flank was instructed to attack.

The men in the centre heard the yells and, obeying Lee's earlier order, attacked, but despite pressing their attack most courageously, were cut down by the devastating cannonading of the Union artillery. The units on the left were halted and forced to take what cover they could. Jackson and Ewell moved too late to assist the centre, while the other reserves were never called, and by 9 p.m. the sounds of battle faded to be replaced with the terrible and plaintive cries of the wounded and dying. The Union troops did withdraw that night leaving behind a most grotesque scene: bits of the human body were flung everywhere, heads yards from their former bodies, trunks with no extremities, corpses assuming many weird and bizarre postures.

For this day's work the Confederate loss was 5,355; the Union had suffered 397 dead, 2,092 wounded and 725 missing.

The Confederate did celebrate the seven-day battle yet mourned the price. In total, during this period Lee lost 20,614, a quarter of his command; of this 875 were missing or captured, the rest dead or wounded. The Union tally was 15,849 which included the staggering figure of 6,053 missing or captured.

McClellan had saved most of his command, but to what end? Methinks he may have been intimidated by the image of a force greater than it really was; the Confederates seemed to have borrowed the technique of the European armies.

The Union force took rest at Harrison Landing, a little south of Malvern Hill, with both armies now facing hot weather and the dreaded malaria, present in the swamp areas.

From newspapers the verdict was that neither side had done enough. In the Union the resolve was now dissipating, further aggravated by Democrats and Republicans openly quarrelling and each blaming the other for not capturing Richmond when they had the chance.

The Confederates' problem was to replace more than seventy-six experienced and valuable officers lost in battle while still under threat from McClellan at Harrison Landing to the south, and McDowell to the north of the capital. The call was now out to abandon the political reason to stay on the defensive in order to brand the Union the aggressor. The time had come to be aggressive.

I understand Lee has returned to Richmond to refurbish and reorganize, there being too many divisions to handle efficiently as each tended to be a small army, functioning as such. He was prevented from achieving the revised structure by a Confederate law which states that no force shall exceed a division in size, thus permitting state governors to retain control of the units formed in their state.

While government debated, the Richmond army was provisionally reformed into two commands – I did note the military community diligently avoided the word 'corps'. Longstreet is to lead the first command. The five division commanders are to be Major Generals Anderson and Jones, also Brigadier Generals Wilcox, Kemper and Hood, while the second command is to be led by Jackson and the two division-commanders are to be Brigadier Generals Winder and Ewell. Lee's third command is to be under his personal direction, with cavalry to be led by Jeb Stuart and the three brigade-commanders to be Brigadier Generals Hampton, F. Lee and Robertson.

The next task was to consider the position of officers of the lower ranks in the light of recent performances. This resulted in Magruder's relegation to the dubious, less-important western theatre, although this seems a shame after his valiant ploys against McClellan – the east's loss and the west's gain, methinks. The elderly Holmes and Huger were also transferred to the west.

There was a rift, almost a scandal, in the command; mischief-making I suspect between two rival papers, the *Examiner* and *Whig*, one praising Hill, the other Longstreet for certain deeds in the seven-day battle. It is rumoured that Lee only just managed to prevent a duel.

I received news from Washington that all was not well: it is said that whereas President Davis trusts his commander-in-chief, President Lincoln does not trust McClellan, his commander-in-chief, a situation that has been brought about by Lincoln's anxiety to conclude the conflict, and by a renewed advance from McDowell in the north and McClellan from the south, thus trapping the lesser Confederate army. Despite his urging, all the President received were messages: firstly for an additional 50,000 troops, and soon after for a further 100,000. It seemed that McClellan was still obsessed in overestimating the enemy army, which defect had plagued him ever since he had taken command.

The Union military hankered after a yet larger army, but faced a problem as Secretary Stanton had closed down the recruitment centres, so the President, with the aid of Secretary of State Seward, petitioned the sixteen state governors for 300,000 volunteers. Should the Union army reach this size it would represent a massive challenge to the Confederacy; how they could match it I am unsure. Can Lee give the south a miracle? He will have two or three months before the enlarged Union army can possibly come into action.

Sir, I shall close this letter and dispatch it. There are further rumblings from the Union military, and I wish to undertake a brief trip to Washington to glean what facts I can.

I will write on my return to Richmond.

Sir, I am, and remain, your obedient servant . . .

Richmond
15 August 1862

Sir,

The matter in Washington took longer that I envisaged, the prime difficulty being to obtain reliable facts. What I am about to relay to you may sound familiar; I refer to the play, *Macbeth*, by our illustrious writer.

An Irishman did have a quaint term for the happenings, referring to it as political shenanigans. When the Peninsular enterprise was completed, the President and Stanton assumed the joint role of commander-in-chief, officially to release McClellan who could then give his full attention to the enterprise in hand. My opinion is that he was relieved because of his poor showing from November 1861 to March 1862 while occupying that position. Secondly, he was responsible for many delays, seeking as he did to ever enlarge the army under his command. It is claimed that when he did receive additional troops he did immediately write requesting yet further troops in view of the number of enemy troops facing him, which always turned out to be grossly exaggerated.

I was informed that Major General Pope was recalled from the western command, arriving post-haste in June having gained the reputation of possessing a zest for battle. He will now command a new force to be known as the Army of Virginia – the Confederacy should take note of the significance of that name. Pope's command comprises McDowell's corps, divided between Fredericksburg and Manassas Junction, and the corps of Banks and Fremont in the Shenandoah Valley, between Winchester and Middletown. However, it seems that nothing goes smoothly: Fremont resented a junior now being in command and thus resigned, so Major General Sigal was given Fremont's command. Pope became a willing accomplice of Stanton's in an effort to cause McClellan's fall from favour and diminish his popularity.

In mid-July General Halleck was recalled to Washington to fill the post of commander-in-chief, and his command in the west was reorganized. Grant had command of 67,000 men, the object being to capture Vicksburg while Buell was given the task of clearing east Tennessee. The President did travel to Harrison Landing on 7th July to carry out a personal assessment, resulting from the anti-McClellan campaign, but little was gained: some commanders favoured a withdrawal while others desired once again to attempt the capture of Richmond. In the two weeks that followed, McClellan made his own situation worse by not offering any plans, yet still continuing to seek extra troops.

Halleck did visit McClellan, and seemingly spurred him to offer to advance on the rebel capital. However on 3rd August the President did order Halleck to withdraw the army from the Peninsula – welcome news for Lee. Pope did not endear himself to his command, indicating that there would be no more hiding behind defences: the troops were to look forward not backwards, as success and glory are in the advance. This proclamation did not sit well with the troops and commanders and when he signed orders with the term 'Headquarters in the saddle', he became an object of ridicule. The joke was that he did not know his headquarters from his hindquarters. There is still witticism in the ranks, even in time of conflict. He also upset the Virginians by declaring that Union troops would live off the land, causing apprehension among some generals who feared this might encourage the troops to rob as they pleased. Furthermore, he stated that a citizen caught in the act of an attack on Union soldiers or properties would be executed. Surely this is not within the rules, that war should be waged against the civilians. Woe betide the General should he fall into Confederate hands, for he will surely receive short shrift. That concludes the events in Washington.

In Richmond I can report a change has taken place with respect to the western command. Beauregard did assume command after Johnston's death at Shiloh, but fell out with President Davis and was replaced by General Bragg. It is said the man suffers from various ailments that manifest themselves from time to time, otherwise he is considered a promising officer.

Now I wish to report the happenings to date. After their mauling at Fort Pillow, the Union fleet did once more attempt the downriver passage, and on 6th June another battle did take place against the Confederate flotilla. One Confederate ship sank, while two others collided and ran aground. Four more were put out of action, leaving only one, the General Van Dorn, to escape downriver. The Union's only fatality was Colonel Ellet who died from an infection. The city of Memphis had no choice but to surrender immediately after the encounter. The Union force moved down to anchor north of Vicksburg when Farragut made his second attempt against the city, as I wrote you. On land 3,200 troops face 10,000 Confederates.

Meanwhile the Confederates had constructed a monster armoured vessel named *Arkansas*. This warrior did sweep down and surprised the Union fleet on 15th July, scoring hits on most of the ships and disabling one. The Union fleet suffered seventeen dead and forty-two wounded, while on the *Arkansas*, human remains were splattered everywhere from the twelve dead men and eighteen wounded.

Farragut's pride had been hurt. He thus ordered the fleet to run past Vicksburg and anchor downstream, each ship in turn firing on the *Arkansas* as they passed, but despite their efforts the gunboat *Winona* was beached, leaving the *Arkansas* unscathed.

The battle was not yet over. The ironclad *Essex* and the *Queen of the West* were sent against the *Arkansas* on 22nd July. However, sickness was plaguing the Union troops, and by the end of July Farragut had to abandon any attempt against Vicksburg. The troops recuperated at Baton Rouge, but whilst there were attacked by a Confederate force of 2,600. Many Union officers were killed including their commander, Brigadier General Williams. The plan was that the *Arkansas* would attack the Union ships but she failed to appear, and the next day self-destructed, thus the gunboats did halt what might have been a Confederate victory. The Union suffered 383 losses and the Confederates lost 456; President Lincoln's brother-in-law, Lieutenant Todd, was one of the dead.

One of Halleck's acts was to reduce Grant's army to 100,000, comprising the Tennessee command and Rosecrans, and 67,000 of the Mississippi command. Buell's 101,000-strong army of Ohio men moved to Kentucky to watch Bragg. Now Grant, with his forces stretched from Memphis through Corinth to

Luka, could only sit and guard his little area of south-west Tennessee.

News has been received about a small exploit by the Union. On 8th April, General Mitchel marched out from Nashville to occupy Huntsville in Alabama. To prevent a Confederate reinforcement of Chattanooga he had a fellow by the name of Andrews to help him to destroy certain bridges. Andrews and his henchmen were finally captured and hanged as spies.

Huntsville was captured on 11th April, with 200 taken prisoner. From there General Mitchel occupied lengths of track in both directions, placing him near Decatur and Stevenson, thirty-five miles west of Chattanooga, holding a vital section of railway, but Buell did not send reinforcements. This was during the period when Halleck was taking Corinth. Mitchel's men terrorized the local populace whenever the telegraph wires were cut or trains fired on, threatening to burn houses and kill all the men. Another disgrace was at Athens, when the men were allowed to run amok as a reprisal. Buell was released after the capture of Corinth to proceed to Decatur and the Cumberland Gap, thereafter to consider an advance against Atlanta, but Mitchel had destroyed a bridge too many; this one was essential to Buell, if he were to supply his 31,000 army. This was the start of a jinx on him.

The railway lines were in disarray, as much from Mitchel's work as from the Confederates. When Buell arrive in Athens on 27th June, supplies from Nashville were in chaos and had to be rationed. To compound his misfortunes, the River Tennessee was low owing to the hot dry weather. The matter was worse when Buell arrived in Huntsville, where he discovered many offences against the populace, whom he did not wish to alienate. He court-martialled the officer responsible for the sacking of Athens, but the culprit responsible for the burning of Paint Rock escaped justice. Corruption abounded when the rogue was pardoned and actually promoted by those in Washington.

Now to two events which have come to my notice and serve to prove the worth of cavalry in this vast land. The Confederates do have two forces: one of 56,000 men at Tupelo, commanded by Bragg and the other of 10,000 men at Chattanooga, commanded by Smith. Smith had to face Mitchel to his west, another 9,000 troops to the north and Negley, with 6,000, from the north-west. Negley fired on Chattanooga on 7th June and then withdrew. On 4th July, Morgan, with a Confederate cavalry force of 990 left to cause havoc between Nashville and Louisville, arrived in Sparta after riding 104 miles in three days.

Here he recruited 200 men, increasing his force to 1,100. Next he attacked Tompkinsville, achieving personal satisfaction when he captured Major Jordon. This fellow had insulted the good womenfolk of Lebanon when the Union force did occupy the village. Now Jordon was sent packing to prison in Richmond. After a brief exchange of musket fire the 400 Union men were paroled and Jordon's fate was sealed. That encounter took place on 7th July when, thirty miles from Tomkinsville, he did cause panic and confusion among the Union military, with bogus reports. To add to the panic, Morgan appeared near Louisville. Alarms were raised in the whole of the Ohio Valley, in Cincinnati and Louisville. Arriving in Cynthiana on 17th July, Morgan, did take many prisoners and capture 300 horses; few Union soldiers escaped after the exchange of fire.

In just three weeks Morgan and his 1,200-strong force had ridden 1,000 miles, captured seventeen towns, destroyed or turned over to local people the Union properties seized. He had also taken 1,200 prisoners. A particularly satisfying factor was that he had put a stop to plans by the Union, for a while at least, to attack Chattanooga. However, conflicts are never fair and Morgan's efforts brought volunteers flocking to the Union army from Kentucky, Indiana and Ohio. Ironically the recruitment officers did cheer Morgan.

On 6th July, Smith did send out another cavalry force of 1,000, commanded by Forrest, whose objective was to capture the important depot of Murfreesboro. On 12 July, Forrest halted in Woodbury. En route Wharton's Eighth Texas regiment and Lawton's Second Georgia regiment had linked with him, plus companies and battalions from Georgia, Tennessee and Kentucky, and troopers who seemed not to be part of a regiment.

At Woodbury it was learned that the Union had rounded up many men and imprisoned them in Murfreesboro. Forrest acted. After reviewing the situation his plan for dawn was thus: Wharton was to engage the Union troops on the outskirts; Hood to head straight for the prison and other key buildings with the aid of Morrison; and Lawton to circle the town to the west and stop any advance by the second encamped Union force. Wharton and the Union commander, Duffield, were both seriously wounded in the exchange of fire. The Union force retreated behind a fence and stood their ground, the Confederates being content to keep them pinned down by musket fire. In the meantime Union warders tried to shoot their prisoners then burn the rest; however the Confederates rescued most of them. General Crittenden and his staff were captured at the hotel and the courthouse had to be stormed to overpower some Union soldiers who were holding out there. Meanwhile Union and Confederates faced each other west of the town.

Forrest, on noting the situation, devised a cunning plan. He went to where Wharton had a Union force pinned down, threatening not to take prisoners, and informed the unfortunate officer that all other Union forces had surrendered. With these troops taken prisoner, Forrest then returned to the other front where he contrived to give the impression that he had a very large force, thus intimidating the poor Union officer into surrender. Forrest had it all. His booty included 1,200 prisoners, fifty wagons, a battery of cannons, and a quarter of a million dollars' worth of supplies.

Buell was infuriated and sent a force of 3,500 to repair the damage and stop Forrest. The force did repair the damage but failed to stop Forrest, who struck near Nashville on 21st July, destroying three bridges and taking ninety-seven prisoners. The Union force was unable to repair these bridges for many days.

There seems to have been manipulation afoot by Smith; he is a restless man and misses the glory of his past exploits at Bull Run, and other incidents. There is ambition behind the present series of alarmist letters and requests to Richmond, the President, Lee and Bragg, which dwells on two matters: that Buell approaches, making reinforcements necessary, and that Bragg should be responsible for Chattanooga. Bragg, I understand, was also concerned about Grant and the possible threat to Vicksburg, finally sending part of his force to the city and a further force to Smith. This was indeed a feat of logistics, the like of which I have not known before. Bluell blocked Bragg's direct route to Smith so Bragg sent the mounted section, cavalry, wagons and artillery with 5,000 men on a journey of 430 miles south to Tuscaloosa in Alabama, then east to Rome in Georgia, finally north to reach Smith. His remaining force of 35,000 did undertake a 800-mile journey by train: first south to Mobile, then east to Atlanta and finally north-west to Chattanooga. The first train left on 23rd July, and the last on 27th; truly a wonderful feat.

I cannot quite understand how Bragg and Smith intend to achieve their separate objectives: a strike into Kentucky for Smith, and Buell's defeat by Bragg. Bragg's force now numbered 27,000 while Smith commanded 20,000. There is no further news from this quarter.

You will note that I have delayed my visit to New York in view of the changes within the Union and the Confederacy; my

general feeling is that both sides are girding themselves for greater conflict.
Sir, I am, and remain, your obedient servant. . .

Richmond
1 September 1862

Sir,
I have further delayed my visit to New York in order to send you the latest communiqué of the conflict. As I suspected, August has been a month of great conflicts, which I now set forth for you.

Smith and Bragg have both been active. On 14th August, Smith left Knoxville with 6,000 troops, leaving one division to face the Union force in the Cumberland Gap, and on 18th August he arrived in Barboursville. This did cause the Union force to leave the Cumberland Gap and move into eastern Kentucky. On August 24th cavalry units did clash briefly at Big Hill, west of the Cumberland mountains, the Union side quickly retreating. On 28th August, at Smith's suggestion, Bragg moved his force towards Kentucky, to divert Buell's attention. In the afternoon of 29th, a skirmish started near to Richmond, Kentucky, and continued till dusk when Union Cavalry withdrew to Richmond.

I gather bad timing did bring on a battle at Richmond the next day. The Union commander had sent a courier to request instructions; orders to withdraw were given but did not arrive in time. The Confederates did open with cannon fire. The Union were the first to advance on their left but were held. Then at 7.30 a.m. the Confederates did advance on their left and the Union line withdrew after heavy losses, their reformed line soon broken by another Confederate charge. Most of the Union troops were retreating fast into and through Richmond. General Nelson made one last stand with 2,000 men at 2 p.m. Three hours later, the Confederates did attack on all fronts and soon routed the Union, another example of the use of cavalry, which had moved round to the north of Richmond to attack fleeing Union troops. That was enough for the Union troops, who did surrender in large numbers. The toll was as follows: Confederates seventy-eight dead and 372 wounded; Union 206 dead, 844 wounded and 4,000 taken prisoner. The booty included 10,000 arms, nine cannon and a complete wagon train of supplies.

Lexington and the state capital of Frankfort were now Smith's to occupy. From Lexington, it was but a short train ride to

Louisville and Cincinnati, much to the consternation of Washington. In Virginia, Pope was on the move: he positioned Banks towards Culpeper House, on one railway line, thereby threatening Gordonsville. It was also Banks's objective to interrupt the railway there, where there was a link between Richmond and the Shenandoah Valley. While Banks was moving sluggishly on 12th July, Jackson moved his command to Gordonsville on 19th July.

Shortly after noon on 9th August, Jackson and Banks joined battle at Cedars Mount where once again the Confederate tactics proved superior, with about 21,000 men opposing the Union's 9,000. The Union did open fire whilst Jackson prepared his lines and by 4.30 p.m. both sides were making great use of their cannon. Then at 5 p.m. the Union launched a surprise attack in the centre, breaking three lines of defence, and hand-to-hand fighting broke out; it seemed that the entire left wing of Jackson's line had been outflanked. Jackson did personally rally the men, who stood their ground for a while before retreating. By then reinforcements had arrived and pushed back the Union attackers. Winder was wounded and died after the battle. Now, with further reinforcements, the Confederates pushed forward and, despite a valiant effort, the Union was forced to give ground. Finally, Hill did lead a charge and the battle was over at 6.30.p.m. though the Confederates continued to give chase until they encountered a fresh Union division near Culpeper, by which time it was 11 p.m.

Bank's premature attack without reserves did cost him 30 per cent of his command, some 2,377 men. Jackson lost 1,355 men. McClellan started to move back to Fort Monroe on 13th August.

Lee had received news that Burnside was on his way to join Pope at Fredericksville, and had to consider the possibility that McClellan might also be linking up at Fredericksville, which could mean some 130,000 men advancing on Richmond from the north. The entire army, with the exception of 25,000 men left to defend Richmond, began a march north on 15th August, to deal with Pope before the forces had a chance to join together. Each army had about 55,000 men.

Lee sent Stuart and his cavalry to destroy a bridge used in the transportation of vital supplies and during this mission, Stuart was almost captured. However, another officer, who by chance knew of Lee's plans, was captured instead, and Pope quickly moved his troops to prepare for Lee. Confederate cavalry did harry the rear of Pope's army.

On 22 August, Stuart did skirt behind Pope's lines and by

chance attacked his headquarters, discovering details of Pope's plans, naturally of importance to Lee, and revealing that one of McClellan's corps had arrived that day at Aquia Landing, others were soon to arrive at Alexandra. Soon Pope would command 70,000 troops.

Lee had a daring plan that would drive Pope further from Richmond, and possibly deal a severe blow before McClellan's actions could begin to take effect. The plan was this: Jackson, with 25,000 troops plus Stuart's cavalry, was to move north. Meanwhile, to disguise this move, Longstreet, with 30,000 troops was to appear as if he were about to attack Pope.

At 8 a.m. on August 25th Pope knew of Jackson's movement yet was deceived as to the true intent, thanks to Longstreet , and on the 27th, Jackson's force proceeded through an unguarded pass to capture the Union's main supply depot at Manassas Junction – a costly oversight by Pope. The depot covered a square mile. A Union force did foolishly march on the Junction. Both sides were surprised but the Confederates reacted quickly and routed the enemy, taking many prisoners.

Lee, with Longstreet and 30,000 men, headed for Thoroughfare Gap leaving Jackson to take up positions at Stoney Ridge on the northern end of Bull Run, scene of the previous year's battle. I understand disagreements as to how best to use the Washington defence force and the reinforcements, did arise between Halleck, Pope and McClellan. There were also hostilities between division and corps officers regarding loyalties to the various commanders.

News of Manassas reached Pope, who sent a division to investigate the situation. Fighting started at 7 a.m. at Bristoe, continuing all day. The Confederates then returned towards Manassas. Pope arrived and discovered Jackson with a large raiding force which he planned to attack and destroy, thus weakening Lee's army whom he considered would be attempting to march to the Valley. I understand from my military acquaintances that Pope made a blunder in ordering McDowell to advance to Manassas from Centreville. Approaching Thoroughfare Gap Lee and Longstreet's force had to fight a Union force sent by McDowell which had arrived only hours before Lee. Meanwhile the entire Union army was marching hither and thither; shortages of rations and having to sleep on rough ground were taking their toll.

Although McDowell managed to keep out of the way until next day, some of his command were surprised when Jackson attacked them and for several hours the opposing sides did stand seventy-five yards apart firing at each other, each presenting itself as a target to the other. This frenzied fight did last for ninety minutes, resulting in terrible slaughter, yet neither side would yield. Someone's description was that the soldiers appeared to be mesmerised. For that day's work both sides lost 1,300 gallant, brave, but foolhardy men.

That evening Lee did dislodge the Union force at the Gap by a flanking movement. One Union officer, Brigadier General Ricketts, was aware of the advance through the Gap, but had failed to inform Pope or McDowell – no small wonder as both commanders were missing.

August 29th: Jackson had prepared defences between Gainsville and Centreville and although his left flank was being attacked, the Union assaults came to nothing. Noon and Pope arrived along with fresh Union troops numbering 20,000, but they were ineffective. At 3 p.m. a brigade advanced and found an opening in the Confederate line, breaking the first and second lines of defence before the Confederates launched a counter-attack. The Union force was now isolated, attacked on all sides; many uncoordinated attacks by the Union forces had come to grief. At 5 p.m. Kerney did launch an attack on the far left of Jackson's line, pushing back the opposing force some two hundred yards before he in turn was pushed back. By this time the Confederates were extremely low in ammunition and feared they would be overpowered in the next assault. At the last moment reinforcements arrived and the whole sector charged the enemy with bayonets. Porter was ordered to attack Jackson's right flank and, after some deliberation, decided not to take action as by that time the light was poor.

August 30th, and Pope felt victory would be his, contemptuous of McClellan when he received a message from Alexandra requesting cavalry to guard the supply wagons, compounding my impression that there is little love lost between those officers. Pope had the idea that Jackson intended to withdraw so on that morning moved several regiments to prepare for pursuit, little knowing that for the past twenty-four hours Longstreet had been in the vicinity, and leaving just one division to stop him. The Union commander must have been so sure of the Confederates' intent that when informed by Porter of a force confronting him, the information was dismissed. Then Burford's report of enemy troop movement through Gainsville was also dismissed; even the clash between Hatch's and Hood's forces was ignored. When a courier returned from Rickett, at the right of the Union line, and reported that the enemy was pressing, he still took no action.

Porter, Hatch and Reynolds advanced from the Union centre to encounter the full might of Longstreet, and when Reynolds did gallop to Pope and reported the matter, Pope believed it to be nothing of importance. How strange it is when commanders become obsessed with an idea, stranger still how some officers firmly believed that Jackson had gone; they were in for a rude awakening. Even odder was McDowell's action in moving much of his force from his left, leaving but a token force of 1,000 men and six cannons to face Longstreet.

Porter did now advance against an entrenched enemy, sustaining terrible losses from the guns of the Confederates. Having reached the entrenchment, one Union officer, Major Barney, did urge his men from the front and was shot to death for his deed. Likewise when the Confederates did counter-attack, Colonel Baylor was struck down in similar fashion. Now the hitherto-concealed Longstreet opened up with cannon and caused great destruction to Porter's force before moving forward in full force. Line after line of Union troops managed to fire only one round before being engulfed by a flood of grey uniforms. The tide swept on and next captured the guns of Captain Kerns, which valiant gentleman did die with his guns when all others had fled. At 6 p.m. Jackson began to move forward the left end of his line. Pope had to reorganize his line, which he established at Chinn Ridge and Henry House Hill.

By 5.30 p.m. the Union force were already being hard pressed from two sides on Chinn Ridge, and Texans and Virginians combined to storm Chinn Ridge, routing the Union defenders and seizing further guns. Few units did face the tidal wave of grey, but in the end they also had to yield or be annihilated. The tidal wave rolled on to Henry House Hill, not halted by the Union battery. Union troops at the base of the hill in turn also had to give way, so only the force at the crest stood in the Confederates' way.

Just before sunset the Confederates did bombard the hill and then attack, but had not succeeded by 8 p.m. when rain began to fall.

Pope's beaten army retreated across Stone River and, for the second time, across Bull Run River, heading for Centreville and Washington. Lee had already inflicted much humiliation on Pope, yet there was one further blow he intended to deliver. Jackson's tired force set off to cut off Pope's retreat at Centreville.

News has only just reached me that one further brief and bloody encounter did take place at Chantilly, in a thunderstorm to boot when two Union commanders were killed: Stevens of the 79th New York, and Kerney, respected by many fellow officers, friends as well as foe. His death did remind me of the story of when officers had to choose sides, future enemies bidding each other farewell and good fortune.

As for Pope and some of the other officers, I suspect they will be transferred out of harm's way. My guess is that McClellan, who did contrive to keep out of the battle, might well replace Pope: death is not the only price; dishonour is a far worse burden to carry for the rest of one's life. It would indeed be a strong man who could overcome such an affliction.

The cost of this enterprise is thus: Union, 14,462, 4,000 of whom were taken prisoner; Confederates, 9,474. I have one other comment regarding McClellan. It is said he is loved by the army, and can do anything with the men except lead them to victory. I wonder as to his future.

Sir, I do trust that the map I sent you has been of value. I have in my humble way tried to describe the circumstances and situations of these various conflicts so that you can gauge the true intent of the two combatants and maybe determine the strengths and weaknesses and whether luck favours one against the other.

For the time being I shall stay in Richmond to learn of Lee's future intent, which should place me in a better position when I undertake the visit to New York.

Sir, I am, and remain, your obedient servant. . .

Richmond
1 October 1862

Sir,

An announcement was made today that General Beauregard took up his appointment as commander of Charleston on 15th September. This is in response to newspaper reports that Washington is preparing to attack that city, although I suspect they have not taken into account the amount of fortifications there; it would be like a fly landing in the very middle of a spider's web. I know from my last visit that the place is a military stronghold held by determined people, and any Union commander who undertakes this enterprise may well risk his career.

Firstly, I will inform you of the situation in the west. Buell is spending time protecting his supply lines while waiting for Braxton to make clear his intent. On 12th August the

Confederates did raid Gallatin, destroying the depot and bridges and blocking a tunnel to interrupt the flow of supplies from Louisville to Nashville. Bragg moved out of Chattanooga on 28th August towards Sparta, in Kentucky. Buell remains confused about enemy movements, arriving with the army in Murfreesboro on 5th September to find a paucity of provisions. Two columns of Confederates were now in Kentucky. Polk marched beyond Sparta and occupied Glasgow on 14th September.

Buell moved yet again, through Nashville to reach Bowling Green, just thirty miles west of Glasgow, on the same day as Polk arrived.

Bragg's move had enticed the Union force out of Alabama and central Tennessee, and while gathering all his forces, he sent a small force north to cut off the railway at Cave City. This was completed without incident, then the unpredictable happened: the officer-in-charge elected to attack Munfordville and received a bloody nose for his endeavours. Bragg had to move against the force and it wasn't until the 17th that a surrender took place.

Now started a bizarre dance between two armies, conducted in a drought-ridden land with little in the way of supplies and little food to be had from foraging. Methinks if I had been a soldier in either army I might be asking what the generals were about: all the seemingly pointless marching with little in the belly. I feel the soldier would at that moment have preferred a good fight and be done with it.

From the information I have, events were thus: Buell moved tentatively towards Munfordville on the 18th and then marched to Louisville, to arrive on the 25th. On 1st October he set out with 60,000 men towards Bardstown, having had problems while in Louisville. Firstly, he had to resolve issues with Washington, who was to assume overall command, as the commander in Louisville did not come under his authority. Next, General Nelson was shot dead by Brigadier-General Davis; thirdly, Major General Thomas was to supersede Buell on instructions from Washington. Thomas declined, but became second-in-command.

Bragg marched to Green River and on 20th marched to Bardstown, he or Smith having had little success with volunteers. Bragg then devised a plan whereby if he were to install Lieutenant Governor Hawes in the state capital of Frankfort, he could then conscript men.

That is the news to date. All here in Richmond are expecting an imminent clash.

In northern Mississippi there are two Confederate forces: Major General Price with 17,000 men in Tupelo, fifty miles south of the important Union base of Corinth, and Major General Dorn with 10,000 men at Holly Springs, fifty miles west of Corinth. Price seized Luka on 14th September, providing him with plenty of bounty. Grant's aim was to destroy Price before he could link with Dorn and attack Corinth. Ord advanced along the north road towards Price while Rosecrans' forces marched along the two southern roads, timing being all-important as Ord was to delay his attack from the north until he heard Rosecrans begin his attack. Then fate intervened to put asunder the well-laid plan: Rosecrans did engage around 2.30 p.m., but the weather prevented the sound of battle carrying to Ord. Price had his main force facing Ord and quickly moved against Rosecrans. A seesaw fight began around a Union battery which changed hands several times. During the night Price slipped by Rosecrans on a road parallel to the Union force and was then able to link with Dorn. The losses: Union 825, including 141 dead; Confederate 693, including 86 dead.

Methinks we shall soon hear of a conflict at Corinth, which could cause considerable problems to the Union in its Mississippi venture. In such a short time Lee has beaten two Union armies who were stronger, better equipped, and better fed.

News did break on 10th September that Lee was marching into Maryland; what other general could possibly have shown such enterprise? To this day no other commanding officer has acted in this manner, be he Union or Confederate.

One of my military acquaintances did explain to me the objectives: Lee would not permit the Union to reorganize so as to endanger Richmond again. To directly attack Washington, only twenty-five miles to the west, when outnumbered two to one, was not wise, especially against a fortress. There was little left to forage when the army now rested, so it was not practical to stay. Withdrawal to Richmond would merely invite another attack, but by invading Maryland Lee could harass the enemy and feed the army and animals from the rich autumn crops, leaving Virginia to carry out the harvest in peace. He could lure the enemy from Washington, ensuring there would be insufficient troops to mount another drive on Richmond.

As well as the military advantages, there were also excellent political advantages. There was pro-Confederate sympathy in Maryland but the state was forced to stay in the Union whereas this move would provide the chance for men to join the southern states. Many people in the Union were showing signs of anti-war attitudes, the Democrats being the most vocal. In November the President faces an election, and even if he were re-elected the hue and cry might be so great that he would have to abandon his previous policy.

I have heard that since the recent victories, several European nations are considering recognition of the Confederacy. Surely we can but wish Lee every success, so that within a few months this whole ghastly business can be concluded. It would give me great pleasure to pursue the company's objectives, come the start of a new year. The company would grow as rapidly as the Confederacy, especially if some of those states, at present restrained, join to swell the Confederacy.

Lee crossed the Potomac at White Ford, on 4th September and was beset by two problems. More than 15,000 men did leave for numerous reasons. Many were near their homes and so it was only to be expected after all they had suffered since the outset. However Lee received 20,000 fresh troops, his force now numbering 50,000. The other problem was disputes between Hood and Evans and between Hill and Jackson. Lee himself had injured both his hands, yet nothing withstanding, the army was cheerful at the prospect of the forthcoming expedition. To be on enemy soil made a change, and they had the added knowledge that they had many friends in the state. The army passed through Leesburgh and finally completed its crossing on the 7th.

The good citizens of Richmond read with pleasure of the scenes in Washington since the battle on the previous Sunday. There had been such panic in the military command regarding the defeat that a farmer galloped down Pennsylvania Avenue, yelling that the Confederates were coming. Pandemonium was rife and hasty plans made to evacuate the President by ship. The people of Richmond were especially amused by the extent of the chaos, which was simply due to Lee having crossed the Potomac.

Sunday 7th, and Lee's army encamped near the city of Frederick, a mere twenty-five miles from the Union base at Rockville.

How remiss of me: I did omit to inform you of the news that a Confederate army was massing near Cincinnati, causing further wailing in Washington. If there had ever been a black day this was it.

McClellan did act swiftly and in no time had 80,000 men on the march to meet Lee. The first clash between forward units happened late on the 8th when Union troops were repelled.

Lee now moved, firstly to remove the 12,000-strong Union garrison at Harper's Ferry and 2,500 at Martinsburg (and to this end Jackson was to capture Martinsburg) then to help at Harper's Ferry. McLaws was to confront Harper's Ferry from the Maryland side while Walker was to approach from the Virginian side. Longstreet would set off for South Mountain and Boonsboro. The army moved on the 10th, leaving behind many false trails for the citizens to repeat when Union troops arrived.

Jackson, as usual, took a devious route through Boonsboro and Williamsport, before turning towards Martinsburg.

Meanwhile McClellan did march slowly, six miles a day, and thus on the 11th was still fifteen miles from Frederick. Halleck was also concerned and cautious, fearing that Lee's movement was merely a feint and that the real drive would come from Virginia, directly at Washington, now greatly depleted. Again McClellan was suffering from his old obsession with numbers; it was claimed that Lee had 100,000 men, and even his own intelligence estimated the figure to be 200,000. Then another of those fateful events occurred. A copy of Lee's plan was discovered by accident by a soldier in a field, and was passed to McClellan.

Jackson had forced the 2,500 troops out of Martinsburg on the 11th and they were now at Harper's Ferry, ready to join the other 11,500. The Confederate force was 21,000.

McClaw deployed his force on the 12th: one section to guard his rear at Brownsville Gap, one section to seal any escape route from the Ferry, and the rest to seize Maryland Heights. They finally dislodged the 1,700 defenders on the 13th, and by now the Union force was surrounded. The Union attempted to break through Lee's line at South Mountain on the 14th and were initially successful, but were forced back by the reinforced Confederates. McClellan now brought up his full force and did attack at three points: Turner Gap, Fox's Gap and Crampton's Gap. The Confederates held Fox's Gap, but gave ground at the other two; two officers to fall were the Confederate Garland and the Union Reno.

Lee withdrew that night having prevented McClellan from relieving Harper's Ferry. Jackson, in the meantime, had captured Harper's Ferry, along with seventy-three cannon, 13,000 small arms and 12,500 prisoners.

The Confederate forces regrouped at Sharpsburg, near the Antietam, and when Jackson joined them the odds were two to one against them. By the 16th there were assembled 70,000 Union and 40,000 Confederates.

At dawn on a wet morning Hooker started the advance, and thereafter the battle did flow first one way, then the other, Hooker attacking Jackson's line. Duryee, Seymour, Christian,

Hartsuff and Doubleday pushed back the Confederate commands of Lawton and Jones, and Hood who then threw back the Union force but in turn was stopped by Meade. By 9 a.m. the fighting had subsided but even so 16,000 soldiers lay dead or wounded, an equal amount from each army.

Sumner now advanced as the wounded Hooker was taken to the rear. However Lee had set a trap: while a small number held the front a large force of Confederates did attack the Union flank, and by 9.45 a.m. the Union had suffered great loss and retreated. By 11 a.m. the Union gave up its attack on the Confederate left.

The battle now shifted to the centre, where furious fighting had erupted, the Confederates holding a strong position known as the Sunken Road. When a Union force managed to break through near the road and start to fire on the defenders the Confederate commander made a blunder and withdrew instead of turning to deal with the new attack. The Union troops now in the Sunken Road were menaced on their right but the attack failed. Longstreet and Hill did rally and slowed the Union advance. Those who set off from the Sunken Road got to within half a mile of Sharpsburg. Then at 12.30 the Union force withdrew to regroup.

At this moment a strange set of events took place. The Union had in reserve in the centre, 3,500 cavalry and 10,500 troops; to the north were a further 12,000 troops. Things were becoming critical for Lee as his army had received a battering, yet was still clinging on. Franklin, with his 12,000 force, wanted to attack again in the woods where Sumner had received such a trouncing. McClellan arrived and agreed with Sumner that it was too risky to attempt and if it failed would endanger the army. Likewise in the centre he would not risk another assault. Thus is demonstrated the difference between the two commanders: Lee, prepared to risk all for victory; McClellan, not prepared to take risks for fear of losing. At the southern end of Lee's line were three bridges across Antietam Creek; across the Creek was Burnside, with 11,000 troops and 50 cannon.

May I at this point interpose with some details that might give a clearer picture. This was to some extent the critical place where Burnside could have struck the decisive blow. McClellan and Burnside had been close friends up to two days before. Burnside, in his post of Wing Commander, was not required, as one of his two corps had been given to Hooker to command. There was also a personality conflict between Burnside and Hooker; you will remember that Burnside had been offered the position of

Commander-in-Chief, but had declined while continuing to behave as if he were Wing Commander, passing on any orders to Cox to deal with. This split command of the corps was the first weakness. The second mistake was not to have examined the terrain, and the third was not being aware of the enemy's weakness. Any attack was considered merely to relieve the centre and the north front.

Order to advance finally came at 10 a.m. Burnside's first attempt failed, as those sent forward got lost because of being unfamiliar with the terrain; it was only on the third attempt that the bridge was secured. A small force of 550 Georgians had kept the Union force at bay until 1 p.m. Only then did they withdraw, because two other Union forces had crossed the creek at other points and were now converging on the small band of defenders. At this time the Union force did halt to await supplies. In the meantime McClellan's obsession was once more affecting him and he abandoned further attempts on the north front. The centre assaults were getting nowhere.

Lee was planning a diversion on the north front to ease the pressure in the centre and south, which attempt was quickly repulsed. All his present reserves were committed, so he called upon A. P. Hill's force, still at Harper's Ferry, who set off at 6.30 a.m. and by 2 p.m. had travelled a goodly distance to be within two miles of the battle.

After several couriers urged him to take action, Burnside finally commenced his attack at 3 p.m. One force was halfway to the town when it encountered the Confederates and slowly pushed back the defenders to within 200 yards of the town, where they were halted. A second force began its advance west and, having overcome a mere 700 men, pushed forward before receiving a nasty shock: Hill had arrived at 3.30 p.m and attacked at 3.40 p.m. The surprise favoured Hill, and soon the Union force was pushed back, including the reinforcements who were rushing to stem the retreat.

Burnside was back at the bridge by 5.30.p.m., and although he still had a force of 8,500 remaining and a two-to-one advantage, he did not counter-attack. Hill considered it wise not to press his men after such a march and fighting for two hours, thus the south front was a stalemate. There was one further strange twist before the battle finally abated soon after 5.30 p.m. A keen Union officer had observed the weakness of the Confederate centre, and reported this to McClellan: one final assault, and victory would be theirs. The commander initially agreed, until Porter reminded him he had only limited reserves. The fear that he might yet be defeated by the reckless Lee must have been in his mind, further fuelled by his other defeats at the hands of this Confederate General. Worse, if he were defeated, who would be left to defend Washington? Only a small force had been left for this task.

Next day neither side seemed keen to continue, and truces were arranged at various sites to attend to the wounded and collect the dead. It was a time to count the cost: Union: 2,108 dead, 9,549 wounded, 753 missing, and nine generals dead along with many officers; Confederates: 1,546 dead, 7,752 wounded, 1,018 missing. They had also lost nine generals and many officers, and the death-toll was increasing each hour as men died of their wounds.

This must rank as the most devastating encounter to date. Around one in four of all those involved had fallen, dead or injured; the injuries were horrific. I do ask myself how can this be – how is it possible for men to walk, then run over hundreds of yards, knowing that facing them are the muzzles of many cannon that could smash their bodies to nothing? If they survive this, they then have to face hundreds of musket barrels that could either kill them outright, or inflict excruciating pain and disablement for the rest of their lives.

The night of the 18th, Lee did begin his withdrawal to the Potomac, wagons and men marching the three miles in drizzling rain. Even though McClellan was aware of the enemy movements and had also received a further reinforcement of 14,000, he did not order a pursuit. The man is a puzzle: this is not the first time he elected not to follow the enemy in hot pursuit. Had he done so, he may well have brought about a conclusion to the conflict. Was his purpose to let them go, to fight another time? Certainly he seems to have a desire to intimidate and threaten, or lay siege, rather than engage in direct conflict.

Or is he a man of conscience who sees no sense in a futile loss of life? McClellan is a Democrat, and no doubt subscribes to the same view as others of the party, preferring a negotiated solution to the problem, and to resolve the slave situation slowly and with considered care. The Democrats have no desire to inflict great damage and privation on fellow human beings in the south; in the long term this would not be beneficial to them or to the people.

On the 19th, Lee had the bulk of his army safely across the Potomac, the elderly Major General Pendleton remaining on the Maryland side with forty-four cannon and 600 men to act as a rearguard. Porter had been sent to check on Lee. The two groups clashed around 8 a.m., starting with an artillery duel, spasmodic fighting continuing all day. Some Confederate cannon were captured. Pendleton did ride and report the situation to Lee. Next morning Jackson attacked the Union force near Shepherdstown, and by the end of that day Union men were falling off the bluff into the river far below, to drown or be killed in the river, This was a nightmarish repeat of the nearby massacre at Ball's Bluff eleven months ago. Methinks this did dispel any notion by McClellan to move into Virginia.

While a large force did reoccupy Harper's Ferry, the rest of the Union army stayed in Maryland. The army had one satisfaction: this was the first time they had truly forced the Confederate army to retreat.

At this point I need to comment on the happenings in Washington. On 24th September, President Lincoln issued a proclamation declaring the emancipation of slaves. Please note, this does not apply to the Union slave-states of Kentucky, Maryland, Delaware or Missouri. Many here in Richmond do say that President Lincoln wishes to cause mischief and harm among the people by provoking unrest and revolt among the slaves, one of the major assets to the prosperity of the Confederacy. Many are angry that the Union states are to be excused this proclamation, declaring that this truly shows malice on the part of President Lincoln, and that it would be a woeful time should he be the victor and once more enslave all the people in the south under his despotic rule.

To enable me to consider the best policy for the company, I would ask to be informed of the British and French governments' attitudes towards the recent military action and the proclamation. Here I am able to sum the situation as follows: outrage in the south, anger among the Democrats in the Union, and joy among the abolitionists. I suspect this could be no more than a political ploy by President Lincoln to win the argument, and bring back into the Union the errant states by whatever means are at his disposal. The man has shown the ability to achieve his goals by stealth, and patience, manipulation and ploy, on many occasions.

Malicious rumours are circulating in Washington that McClellan, because of his beliefs, did conspire with Lee. The problem is that those spreading this rumour may have plausible reasons to support the accusation. There is a story printed here that a member of Halleck's own staff, a certain Major Key, stated that McClellan's game was not to destroy Lee's army, the object being that neither side should achieve an ultimate advantage, because it was better that both sides be kept active until exhausted. Then, and only then, will it be possible to compromise and retain slavery. The officer was made an example of by Lincoln. Is there a despot lurking within the President?

I shall conclude this letter as I am anxious to learn of news from Europe regarding the situation here. The issue of the proclamation seems to leave no uncertainty as to the resolve of one man in the Union.

Sir, I am, and remain, your obedient servant. . .

Richmond
15 October 1862

Sir,

I have received your letter today and do note that you had already anticipated the request in my letter, which by now should be safely delivered into your hands.

My policies for the company's work here will have to be radically re-examined in the light of Britain's and Frances's intentions of remaining neutral, and their favourable response to President Lincoln's proclamation. My letter will be brief in view of the above.

Lee has based his army at Winchester, in the Shenandoah, thirty miles south-west of Sharpsburg, and the only movement is from the state of Mississippi. On 19th September there was a battle at Luka, near the Union base of Corinth, as already reported in a previous letter. My prediction regarding a Confederate attack on Corinth did come to pass; of this and other details I shall write further at the end of the month.

In view of the circumstances I consider it prudent to travel first to Washington to discover more of the Lincoln–McClellan situation. Yet more changes in the command of the army can buy the Confederates time to change the present adverse conditions and, more importantly, regain the confidence of Europe.

It is then my intention to visit Mr Withring in New York and reappraise the situation. I am hopeful we may be able to make progress in the company's enterprises and will prepare an agenda. After this, if there is a cessation of military activities with the onset of winter, I hope to be able to meet with Mr Wilbourforce in Montgomery, subject to the availability of functioning railways; so much rail-track seems to be continually uprooted by both protagonists.

Sir, I am, and remain, your obedient servant. . .

Ten
What next?

Washington
30 October 1862

Sir,

There has been a change in the atmosphere here, euphoria and expectancy supplanted by a weariness and despair as to where it is all leading. In privacy a number of acquaintances have confided their disillusionment with events to date. What has happened to the boast that the mighty and stronger Union would deal the errant fellows a sound hiding and have them back in the fold within six months? That now seems so long ago. Others do say, but not openly for fear of bringing down on themselves the wrath of the administration, that those responsible did totally underestimate the resolve of the Confederacy. It is said that the south has far more to strive for, and many do secretly admire the endurance of the people. Even members of the military do respect some of the Confederate generals, especially Lee. Many agree there is no other general in either army with daring, skill and tenacity to match Lee's. I was astonished to hear that it is the declared ambition of some to have the opportunity to oppose Lee before the hostilities are over; to do so, win or lose, would be counted as an honour.

Officers who have done battle do compliment the Confederate soldiers on their endurance and great fighting abilities; although poorly dressed and many of them footsore and unshod, they present a fearsome sight that might well unnerve many an experienced soldier. Their yells in particular can send a chill through the soul. Above all the officers respect the bravery of these men, who knowingly charge an enemy twice in number; these Confederates usually face odds of from two-to-one to as many as ten-to-one. Although they invariably withdraw, they act with discipline and coolness and have yet never been whipped.

These views I do tend to concur with, and would go further: to the best of my knowledge, no Union commander has yet been successful in the destruction of a Confederate force. Each time after a bloody account they have slipped away to reform and strike again, like a snake to twist and turn, then suddenly appear and strike.

There have been further clashes which I shall endeavour to relate.

Buell was on the march, advancing towards Bardstown.

Bragg's 22,500-strong army did hold a line some fifty miles long from Bardstown then north-east to Shelbyville, between Louisville and Frankfort. On 2nd October a small Union force was forcing back the Confederates at Shelbyville. Bragg countered this threat by ordering Smith to leave Lexington with his force of 10,000 to join the rest of the army; Polk was to set out to the north and attack the enemy on the march towards Frankfort. However Polk knew that Buell was coming south and withdrew his supply depot and reserves at Bryantsville. Bragg seemed intent on his idea of seeking more troops by conscription once the Confederate administration was installed in Frankfort, on the 4th. I understand the inauguration was short-lived; within hours, a Union force did enter the place. The administration must have been one of the shortest-lived in history, a mere eight hours.

Meanwhile three Confederate forces were on the move: Polk and Hardee were marching south-east from Bardstown, about ten miles apart. Smith was already on the move, coming south from Frankfort. Bragg intended to meet Buell between Frankfort and Harrodsburg. Smith's force was now in that area and did halt. Hardee was having problems with his rearguard, pressed by a Union force. He then moved on the 5th to join Polk, and in doing so left part of his command at Perryville to determine the Union strength. Here seems to be yet another quirk. Buell thought the entire Confederate army was facing him at Perryville, whereas Bragg considered the main Union army to be near him at Harrodsburg.

Union and Confederate cavalry were involved in minor engagements near Perryville throughout the 6th. A greater clash between the infantry occurred on the 7th, when part of one column of the Union army did dispute a water-hole with the Confederates. This was yet another example of combatants choosing the worst possible battleground: the area where the two commanders had come upon each other was in severe drought, and the days extremely hot. All day of the 7th the Union columns were concentrating their forces. The lead column in the centre was on the Springfield track; on the Mackville track, eight miles north, was a second force, with a third ten miles south on the Lebanon track. After two attempts, a Union force gained control of an important ridge.

The next day saw a confusing state of affairs brought about by misconceptions by both commanders. At Perryville, Polk with his 16,000 troops was about to attack a force of 60,000, unaware of the numbers opposing him. Buell, of course, thought his enemy stronger than it was. At Versailles, Bragg had 36,000 facing 12,000 and thought he was facing a far stronger force; and there we have it.

That morning Polk sensed it was no small force ahead of him, and went into a defensive, not offensive posture. Hardee urged Bragg to concentrate all forces in one location, and Bragg actually took command at Perryville around 10 a.m., determined to attack the Union left.

Sir, I trust that these military terms of which I write are known to you.

Strangely Buell had ordered his left and right wings to prepare for an attack at 10 a.m., and timing once again was all-important. The attack was far from ready, and it seemed that Buell would postpone it until the next day, but Father Time did disrupt all the well-laid plans.

The Confederates did bombard the enemy cannon from 12 noon to 1.30 p.m., but no attack was launched as Polk was waiting for an enemy column to join the rest of the Union force first, thinking it better to have a strong enemy in front than a small force snapping at his flank. Finally the Confederate attack started and was held by withering enemy cannon fire. Then it was renewed with vigour, and did storm the enemy cannon and carry on into troops who were just arriving. After some hand-to-hand fighting the Union retreated. Brigadier General Jackson and Terrill, of the Union force, were killed. A mile to the west an attempt to face the onrushing Confederates also failed. Soon afterwards, fresh Union forces drove back the Confederates. Meanwhile the Union centre was under attack and the Confederates had also found a gap between the centre and left wing of the Union line. Finally the Union centre was able to counter-attack and came close to the streets of Perryville but remained there, fearing that if they went further they would be isolated from the main army.

There now arose an important factor: intimidation. The large Union force to the south was afraid of the possible enemy numbers facing them, and thus stayed put all day. Had they known there was only a small number in front of them and attacked, the Confederates would have lost the battle and possibly their army.

By nightfall, both sides held advanced positions within each other's lines, and then nature took a hand. Buell did not hear sounds of battle and had little idea that his army was involved in a ferocious fight, still planning to do battle on the morrow. Polk also had an amusing escapade. Due to the position held by both sides, he came upon one force and ordered it to stop firing at friendly troops. The officer argued that he was firing at enemy troops. Again, an angry Polk ordered a cease-fire and then enquired as to the name of the insubordinate officer and his unit. He must have been truly surprised by the answer and blustered for a while before riding off. Yes sir, in the heat of the moment, Polk had given orders to an enemy force to cease firing on his own troops. This confrontation was truly one of misconceptions, otherwise one side would have been eager to advance and the other retreat.

Buell remained uncertain as to whether or not it was indeed the whole Confederate force facing him, and was not prepared to take the risk. Bragg had finally come to realise that he had taken on the entire army of the Ohio, and so beat a hasty withdrawal that moonlit night to Harrodsburg, to unite his army. The grim reaper claimed a price for this battle of wrong impressions: Union: 845 dead, 2,851 wounded, 515 missing; Confederates: 3,396 dead and wounded.

There was a further change in command when Major General Rosecrans replaced Buell on 23rd October. When challenged as to the reasons why Union troops were not able to march, live and fight like the enemy, the General did retort that his troops did not have the support of the people. The Union army continued on to Nashville, even though the command had changed and there now arose problems of supplies, and of soldiers deliberately surrendering to obtain their paroles. Bragg had reached Knoxville by late October when he was summoned to Richmond by his old friend, President Davis, who was concerned that the adverse remarks against his friend – that he was sane and loyal, but had lost his mind on strategy – were actually directed against him by his enemies.

I have not yet received news regarding the fight at Corinth, my only information being that it took place on the 3rd of this month, and regarding Bragg's visit to Richmond, I will have to await my return there for details.

Now to a matter close to hand. President Lincoln did visit McClellan in Sharpsburg on 1st October. I did overhear one uncouth fellow jest that, 'If old Abe has gone a visiting Mac, then that means he has asked for another 100,000.' His companion did retort, 'Mac hasn't got an army, but 100,000 bodyguards.'

How can ignorant fellows know anything of such matters? They cannot be worthy citizens if they can only snigger, while others do the fighting and the dying.

Commander-in-Chief Halleck did order McClellan to give battle to the enemy on his territory, but McClellan stayed put and conducted a long-range debate, seeking to reclothe and replenish his supplies and animals. Lee was also in dire straits, but had rebuilt his army to twice that at Sharpsburg, two-thirds of McClellan's total force. I heard that there is anger at the army's headquarters because the Confederate Stuart has again traversed the whole length of McClellan's army where it was positioned on the north side of the Potomac.

The President indicated to McClellan that Lee would have to go south and east to get out of the Valley to return to defend Richmond, thus if he, McClellan, went directly to Richmond he should arrive there before Lee. I understand the general set his 110,000 force in motion on the 26th; it appears any remaining rift has been resolved. They did cross downstream from Harper's Ferry and came to a halt at Warrenton. As to Lee's actions, I have no idea.

The only other news relates to the port of Galveston, in the Gulf of Mexico. The reports here in the capital indicate that troops have landed there and occupied the port. The inlets are drying up for the Confederates.

Some time ago, I did write at length about armoured sea-going monsters that were supposedly indestructible. I have learned that the Confederate vessel named the *Merrimac* did blow up when trapped between the blockading ships and troops near Craney Island. This happened on 11th May; so Davey Jones's locker claims another monster of war.

I shall be able to leave for New York within a day.

Sir, I am, and remain, your obedient servant. . .

New York
15 November 1862

Sir,

My journey was uncomfortable, with the onset of winter. I did give a thought for all the soldiers of both sides, as to how they must be faring in their camps; perhaps they prefer the march and battle. Sickness is surely rife for those remote from towns. It seems in these past months many armies of both sides have lived off the land for the best part of the time because wagon trains made slow progress or were unable to keep apace of an advance. Attacks on railways and depots must further aggravate the situation. My prayers do go out to these poor souls.

Mr Withring has been extremely industrious on our behalf, gaining access to the business society and establishing cordial relationships with reputable and less distinguished folk. He has spoken to me regarding an inventory of businesses and names of owners, also the nature of the businesses. We are agreed that this will be useful to you, sir, and to the honourable gentlemen of the Board. I do concur with Mr Withring's opinion that the first priority should be to complete the inventory, which will help us to decide with whom we might be able to enter into partnership. We can offer resources and market facilities in Europe in exchange for reciprocal arrangements in the Union. This information should be delivered to you sir, within the next few weeks. I have asked Mr Withring to send you the details and to also furnish me with a copy.

As to the next matter on the agenda. It is hoped that Mr Withring will be in a position in the early part of the New Year to have completed his investigations into those areas which are weak regarding service or products, and the market conditions for the introduction of new products.

One piece of news just received, relates to another command change; I am not certain whether this will bode well for Lee, or prove a problem. Lee had moved out of the Valley to counter McClellan's move, thus President Lincoln's plan has failed. When the President learned that Lee had reached Culpeper Court House, things happened rapidly as is the way in this country. On 7th November, Burnside did take over command from the relieved McClellan. The outgoing commander did have the opportunity to bid farewell to the army he had created, and this took place on the 10th. I am unsure of the General's future for the rest of this conflict. Perhaps his true gifts might have suited him for the position of president, rather than a soldier.

Sir, I feel my task here is fulfilled and intend to return at the earliest possible moment to Richmond, to be close at hand should a clash between Lee and Burnside come to pass. This might be a vital moment in the history of the Confederacy.
Sir, I am, and remain, your obedient servant. . .

Richmond
8 December 1862

Sir,

Your letter was awaiting me on my return. I have, as you say, been remiss, and shall correct the matter immediately: a letter will be sent to my parents tomorrow. Before departing from New York, I was informed by Mr Withring that his letter should reach you at the London offices before Yuletide.

Now for the long-awaited report of the attack on Corinth.

The Union held the place, which could be defended from a series of earthworks, the first having been constructed during the previous Confederate occupation and located two to three miles from town. The second was close to the town and not as extensive as the first. Rosecrans commanded 22,000 poorly-trained troops; advancing on him was Earl Van Dorn, with an equal and battle-tested force. Dorn received information that to the north-west the outer earthwork was weak, thus Dorn could expect trouble only on reaching the inner earthworks. Unbeknown to him the Union intelligence had intercepted the information before passing it on. When Dorn attacked on 3rd October, it was not as expected. Nevertheless he did overcome the fortification and pressed on to the inner defence. There the Union held, with neither side gaining advantage.

Next day at 10 a.m. Dorn attacked again, his strongest effort against the centre. Against withering cannon fire he succeeded in gaining the earthworks, only to encounter a strong force that had lain concealed. Although taken by surprise and suffering great loss, his force still pressed their attack. By now three regimental commanders were dead. Finally fresh Union troops did cause the valiant attackers to beat a hasty retreat. To the Union defenders' front the whole ground seemed to be covered in grey coats.

Meanwhile Dorn's attack on the Union right had initial success, actually entering the streets of Corinth. Rosecrans did regain the ground by 11.30 a.m., putting Dorn into retreat. Instead of immediate pursuit, as instructed by Grant, Rosecrans considered his troops and rested them that day, setting out the next day, but took the wrong route, thus the two never met.

Grant had a force positioned to cut off Dorn's retreat, but the Confederates simply found another route. Yet again, although there were only small forces involved, the losses were high. Confederates: 4,838 dead, wounded or captured, about one-fifth of Dorn's force. Union loss: 2,839.

Soon afterwards Rosecrans took command of Buell's army.

Dorn did face a Court of Inquiry but was acquitted. However he was transferred to cavalry in northern Mississippi, being better suited to this duty.

There are rumblings about the fate of Vicksburg. It is said that Grant, with his new command, has his sights set on that majestic city. How sad if the finger of conflict should cause distress to the place and its good folk.

On 23rd October Bragg was on his way to Richmond. President Davis was concerned, since there had been so much criticism of Bragg from Polk, Smith, Hardee, Heth and Senator Henry. The army was keen for J. Johnston or Beauregard to lead. Bragg however had things in his favour: the Union had lost 25,000 men, thirty items of artillery, and hundreds of wagons, mules, horses and guns. He still had an army with which to oppose the enemy, although only half its original size. Bragg also had a plan of which the President approved, and therefore returned to his army. President Davis sent for Polk and Smith to discuss the matters of their complaints, and showing great diplomacy, he did promote the two and returned them to Bragg. I wonder whether this was a wise move: time will tell.

Bragg sent General Breckinridge to Murfreesboro with 6,000 men, on 28th October. From there Morgan and Forrest did take their cavalry to do mischief to the Union forces. Rosecrans did beat the Confederates to Nashville, arriving from the Cumberland Gap on 7th November. Bragg's army was in dire straits: illness, lack of food and clothing, with a hard winter ahead of them. Nevertheless he moved on 1st November, first to Chattanooga, then to Tullahoma and on to Murfreesboro, arriving on the 20th. There the army was fed and rested.

President Davis did reveal a scheme to resolve the tension between commanders in the west, while at the same time giving recognition to the western armies. J. Johnston was appointed Commander-in-Chief of the west; Smith joined Bragg's command, renamed the Army of Tennessee; Lieutenant General Pemberton remained in command of Vicksburg. This Johnston is the self-same person I did write about, who was wounded at Seven Pines and did retire, Lee being appointed to his command. It is rumoured that Johnston and the President are somewhat strained in their association since a youthful altercation over a woman, and Johnston is feeling deprived of true recognition.

Johnston arrived to find Rosecrans preparing to move against Bragg and Grant in regards to Vicksburg. His new command appeared to lack many items and was now doubly threatened.

Bragg used his cavalry, as had other Confederate commanders, and sent out on 6th December a force under the command of Morgan, combining infantry with cavalry. Their objective was Hartsville, just thirty-five miles from Nashville. Struggling against snow and extreme cold and crossing the icy Cumberland River, they did attack. After ninety minutes the Union force of 1,834 men did surrender, with prisoners taken and booty destroyed. Someone did say that President Davis has left the capital, but I have no firm information regarding this.

Some time ago I did write regarding the enterprise of the blockade runners; I would request that this matter is considered by the company. The runners have long, sleek, low-lined, and purpose-built ships that are very difficult to detect. With careful planning of tides and moonless nights, it is relatively simple for them to slip through under the very noses of the Union ships, which tend to be at anchor during the night.

Yes, sir, it is true that the Union holds New Orleans, Fort Pulaski to block Savannah, New Bern and Fort Macon, and has recently taken Galveston. Mobile is free but is almost of no use, nor is it easily accessible. There remain only Charleston and Wilmington; these two ports do have an increasing number of Union ships anchored out at sea.

Talking to businessmen here, I understand that the runners are professional and very successful. It is claimed that a ship carrying a cargo of French Cognac, Madeira wine, Belgian silk, perfumes and cigars fetches a handsome price at a port auction; some do say that the profit for one trip can be as high as $425,000, and many can make the run ten or more times before capture. The knowledge of the rivers, estuaries and coastlines plus powerful steam engines that can easily outrun the fastest Union ship – methinks the odds do favour the runner.

I do write of this, sir, should you and the honourable members of the Board wish to consider it as a short-term enterprise. Should this be favourable to you, it might be discreet to inquire of English companies who are involved, with a view to becoming silent partners. It would be advisable to keep quiet about the company's name and its involvement, for if the Union or Confederacy discover this, it might be to the company's disadvantage in the longer term, and any goodwill developed might well dissipate overnight if discovered. This seems a minor risk compared to the profit.

These runners do also have highly-prized and sought-after cotton cargoes destined for Europe. As you are aware, this cotton is of a higher grade than that grown in Asia, and the Union is extremely anxious to also secure it for their mills, which now tend to remain idle for long periods.

My conclusion after a year in this country is clearer than my initial views. Sir, would you consider placing before the gentlemen of the Board, the following policy proposals which, if approved, will greatly assist me in 1863: that the company policy towards the Union, whether victor or vanquished, should be to explore and enter into partnerships, plus limited new enterprises; that the company policy towards the Confederacy, based on its final independence or submission to the Union, should be to explore and develop a host of new enterprises. The area is ripe for development, irrespective of the political outcome, industry and transport being the main areas. There is a readily available, economical labour force, eager for work prospects. There should be no reason now to delay the implementation, at the earliest convenient opportunity, of trade in goods. The present circumstances, which I expect to prevail over the next ten years, dictate that there will be considerable demands for the full range of goods, both basic and luxury.

With the approach of the Yuletide season, I have received many invitations, and will accept as many as is humanly possible with a view to improving my circle of acquaintances who will be helpful to the company.

May I send you, sir, and the honourable gentlemen of the Board, my best wishes for the Yuletide, and may prosperity and good health attend you all for 1863.

Sir, I am, and remain, your obedient servant. . .

Richmond
5 January 1863

Sir,

Greetings and best wishes for 1863.

There is a cautious feeling abroad that a cold and severe winter will deter those who are hell-bent on conflict. Many do pray that the animal instinct in man to cause death and destruction will abate, and that this winter will cool their aggression. Perhaps winter will provide a miracle, and from out of its bosom will grow the seeds of peace and contentment, to be nurtured and reaped for a happy harvest this coming spring and summer.

The celebrations did yield many new acquaintances, all of whom have expressed an interest in the company. No matter how history will treat the Confederacy, everyone agreed that it is time for the south to gird itself and raise the country to the level demanded by the Union; thus if it should stand or fall the goal will still be the same. This is indeed encouraging. However, less encouraging is news of yet further conflict in the last month of the old year. The rumours about the President's departure from Richmond were proved to be correct. He did visit the west to spur his hesitant commanders to action, arriving in Murfreesboro on 10th December. While there he did order 9,000 troops to aid Vicksburg, thus reducing Bragg's force to 40,000 to face an estimated 65,000 force of Rosecrans' in Nashville. The Union also had a further 35,000 guarding the supply lines, with Morgan yet to return from his exploit. In addition Forrest was also away raiding Grant's supply lines in west Tennessee. Morgan was promoted to Brigadier General. President Davis did leave on the 13th to return to the capital.

There is a tale of a young, seventeen-year-old maid named Mattie Ready, who had reprimanded some Union officers when they had occupied Murfreesboro that summer. She was so bold as to declare that she would be the wife of John Morgan, and indeed the gallant Brigadier General did marry the maid during the Christmas festivities; it has been declared as a love match.

Another tale I heard was that the Union commander, Rosecran, received a Christmas present from the Confederates in the form of information that Bragg's forces had been weakened with Forrest away and Morgan away, and 9,000 troops had left for Vicksburg. The day after Christmas, he did move his army towards Murfreesboro, marching in three columns and all taking different routes. Rosecrans seemed so confident that he took only half his force for the fight, around 44,000 men.

No sooner were the Union columns clear of Nashville than they had to stop and take up strategic positions against Confederate cavalry, first at Nolensville, then at Triune and Lavergne. The Union policy of a rapid advance had been thwarted.

By the evening of the 27th Bragg had his forces collected together. The terrain did not favour the defenders; it was rough ground with limestone shelves, boulders, crevices and red cedars. To the west of the town was Hardee, with his line facing north, then Polk in the centre but facing west, his left wing attached to Hardee's line while his right wing was at the River Stone. Across the river and facing north-west was the Breckinridge line. One brief confrontation occurred on the 29th, when a Union force commanded by Crittenden attempted to ford the river and advance into the town. They had received incorrect information and were severely punished for it – Bragg had not retreated.

Confederate cavalry did do mischief to the Union rear

throughout the 30th. Commanded by Wheeler, they came upon a supply train of 300 wagons at Lavergne; he destroyed a million dollars' worth of material and took 700 prisoners. Again, at Nolensville, a similar event took place.

Wheeler's expedition had been bountiful: approximately 1,000 Union soldiers were delighted with their parole, while the Confederates were delighted with the weapons and horses and satisfied with the destruction of four wagon-trains. Rosecrans and his force were now in position to face the Confederates on the 30th. He now tried a deception by lighting many fires beyond his right wing. The day had been one of dismal rain and the night was cool and frosty and, sir, I do relate to you a strange event of that night. A Union band did strike up, playing various popular tunes, whereupon the Confederate band did reply with their own popular tunes, each band listening to the other. Finally the Union band did strike up the well-known tune 'Home Sweet Home', and the Confederate band joined in. This must be the first time that I can recall two armies sleeping the night away, knowing that in the morning there would be a fight, which seems to me to be more in keeping with the practice of European armies. To date, most of the fights seem to have started almost by accident, an initial clash spreading into a major fight as others approached to join the fray. Sometimes they reminded me more of ambushes, the troops emerging from concealed positions.

Reading the accounts I do find the whole thing eerie, taking place on a cold, damp, misty dawn on the last day of a year. Many will not live to see the New Year. On the Union left was a large clump of cedars known as Round Forest; this was transformed into an area of hell.

It is important at this point to mention the styles of the two commanders. Rosecrans tended to be near the front, lending his help at critical points while Bragg commanded from the rear and depended on couriers from the front to decide whether or not an order was necessary. There was danger to both commanders that a battle could be lost if information were not received in time. Another strange factor has come to my notice: each commander's plan was to achieve surprise by striking a first powerful blow. I believe each intended to attack at opposite ends of the line. Bragg's aim was for a quick engagement before Rosecrans could call on the reserves in Nashville, and the 35,000 men on guard duties. Some officers on the Union side sensed something to be amiss at around 2 a.m. when there appeared to be movement in front of them, albeit executed in silence. The corps commander did not seem disturbed by the information, but the officers took precautions and roused the men to eat, then prepare battle-lines. There were others who did reconnoitre but took no further action.

Through the mist at 6 a.m. came the grey-clad figures, ghost-like and moving silently until the last moment, when they uttered that chilling yell. At this point there were several mishaps. One general had left his men to breakfast, while their artillery horses had been taken to the rear for water. One Union regiment that was prepared did advance and engaged in hand-to-hand combat, but finally had to succumb to the greater force. The Confederates now smashed into the unprepared sector, at the same time breaking another section of the line. The Confederates moved round to the flank while their cavalry caused havoc in the Union rear. In the confusion pursued and pursuer became one. Into this came the errant Union officer who chose to give orders to some enemy soldiers and was taken prisoner for his folly.

At this point, two union brigades and most of their cannon were lost. The next section of the Union line did hastily reform to meet the onslaught, standing their ground until the Confederate attack faltered. If they had not, then Rosecrans might have lost his army there and then. Near the centre Polk was attacking and here was yet another mishap, this time on the Confederates' side. Their divisional commander seems to have been intoxicated, sending the first brigade off an hour late, then delaying the second brigade a further hour. Without superior numbers, it was impossible to succeed against a fortified position.

Now to the other end of the line, where Rosecrans set into motion his planned attack. He seemed unconcerned about the noise of battle to his right, or the reported cavalry to his rear, and made the mistake of being over-confident that his commander to the south was coping. Then came some confusing reports from Rosecrans' right, which led him to believe that his commander was holding. Later he realised the predicament and halted his own attack, pulling the troops back into line.

Meanwhile the Confederates were trying hard to break the new Union line on the right, but two mistakes cost them dearly. An advancing force was commanded firstly to cease firing, then told to fire, so that in the confusion they lost the initiative. However the Confederates again managed a flanking movement and the Union line, which now was a V-shape, gave way by 10 a.m. Still the Union position was hammered, until it had to fight while retreating north. By a stroke, the Union ammunition train had been forced to retreat to escape Confederate cavalry, thus the Union force most committed was low on munitions.

To reinforce his left and its advance, Bragg required some of the units on his right. However his right flank had mistakenly thought itself about to be attacked, which was when Rosecrans had halted his proposed advance. The Confederate commander started to advance and found no opposition, but before he could take advantage, sent part of his force to the left. Bragg received a false report of a Union column approaching, thus the force moving left returned to its original position. The centre of the Union V now was pulling back, and those on either side were exposed; however these two forces withdrew a short distance and united to form a new line.

At noon the Union line was centred about Round Forrest and things did abate for a while whilst Bragg moved his right to join the assault there. Polk made the mistake of sending in only two brigades without waiting for the other two to arrive, so two charges were launched, both repulsed by withering cannon fire. The day ended soon after, and in the rain, cold and darkness, men searched out their fallen comrades. It is indeed strange that men can inflict terrible wounds on each other, yet have compassion to help a wounded enemy.

New Year's day dawned and Rosecrans prepared for another day of fighting, while Bragg on the other hand had expected the enemy to have withdrawn. Reports later that morning seemed to confirm they were indeed withdrawing, although what was actually observed were wagon trains removing the wounded to Nashville. Polk moved into the vacated Round Forest, so hotly disputed the previous day; Breckinridge returned to his original position across the Stone River and all seemed relieved when, apart from the odd musket shot or cannon fired off, the day passed without event.

January 2nd started quietly, neither side having moved; the first time such a sequence had happened. It was an unpleasant day, with sleet falling. A cannon duel did erupt near Round Forrest for a while, both commanders having seen a ridge that commanded the whole field of battle; the Union cannons were there first. Breckinridge started his assault at 4 p.m. to gain this important position and succeeded in driving off the Union force, but was in turn driven off, having paid the price of pursuing the enemy force instead of standing on the hill. This incident did remind me of the Battle of Hastings in 1066; now it was repeated in 1863.

The Union side started to build defences ready for yet another assault by the Confederates, knowing only too well the tenacity of the foe. Bragg's force now numbered approximately 20,000, and news of Union reinforcements arriving that morning settled the matter: it was time to withdraw.

What did this cost? For the Union 9,532 dead or wounded from an original force of 41,400; the Confederates lost 9,239 out of a total of 34,732 – a truly staggering percentage for both armies. Polk withdrew to Shelbyville and Hardee to Tullahoma.

Here there has been yet another newspaper attack against Bragg; surely the man cannot survive and Johnston must take command of his force.

There is news regarding Vicksburg and Lee's action there, which I shall endeavour to relate to you in my next letter.

I do now intend to cultivate my new acquaintances and shall report my progress to you in the near future.

Sir, I am, and remain, your obedient servant. . .

Eleven
Experiences

Richmond
10 January 1863

Sir,

It did occur to me after sending my recent letter that the end of this conflict will not be possible for some time yet, at least until a force of arms or common sense will rule the day, but sadly I do not anticipate that day will come this year while politicians and generals remain intransigent.

Under these circumstances I feel you may wish to have the enclosed two maps for future reference. One relates to the western theatre of conflict, the other to the eastern theatre.
Sir, I am, and remain, your obedient servant. . .

Richmond
10 January 1863

Dear Father,

I send you my felicitations for this New Year and trust you are in good health and the estate is prospering.

For myself I am well in body and mind, although the immense size of this country can tire the body and bedazzle the mind on occasions. It is so unlike England, and when you realise that our blessed island can be placed into this country many, many times over it gives an indication of distances.

May I offer you my apologies for the too few letters I have sent you, and hope you will understand when I tell you the best part of my time to date has been in travelling: a portion by train and the rest by wagon and horse, although there were a few times when it was necessary to board a ship because tracks and railways are virtually nonexistent along the eastern seaboard.

The country is amazing in its scenic ranges, and people differ greatly from area to area, although one thing most have in common is their fierce loyalty to their state. They prize it greater than the national government, and seem to have little time or interest in the activities of the body of people in some far-off place.

Newspapers refer to the situation since 1861 as a war, yet to me this is not a war, but a series of conflicts, the purpose of which is unclear to me. It is certainly not to occupy land, because these small opposing forces tend to roam and every so often meet each other, when there is a brief but savage fight after which each side withdraws.

A stranger to this country may find the whole thing a puzzle. A number of states support the original Union of States. Another group of states have formed a Confederacy of States because of their discontentment with members of the Union of States. A third group of states remain independent, or at least not prepared to confirm their commitment to either the Union or the Confederacy. To complete the picture there are great areas of land which are known as Territories because they have yet to form themselves into states.

Since the start of the conflict, most of the forces I referred to have been of 20,000 men or less. Once or twice when Richmond was threatened there were greater numbers, upwards of 100,000 men. But in context it must be remembered these men were spread over many miles that formed the battle front. Of course not all the force would be deployed in the front line, because all good generals prefer to hold some in reserve to meet any unexpected crisis, and I gather from the newspapers that most of the conflicts had several crises during the fighting.

Several interesting facts seemed to have emerged with these conflicts. It is rare for a Confederate force to outnumber an opposing Union force. A fight might start when contrived by the Confederate commander to have the odds in his favour, but these odds quickly change when the Union commander brings up his reinforcements (those reserves I mentioned). To the best of my knowledge it is usual for Union forces to outnumber their Confederate foe by two to one.

The military gentlemen I have spoken with consider that although knowingly faced with these odds, the Confederate soldiers excel because they are fighting on their own soil, and a man fights his hardest in the protection of his own.

It is an amazing thing that although hundreds of soldiers are involved attacking each other, the casualties do not appear to be greater than one-third of the entire force involved. The number of wounded greatly exceeds that of the dead. I did put this question to a military acquaintance. He did explain that it is a rare situation where all the reserves are used, hence if a force has 20,000 men a small portion are used initially to test the enemy and find their weaknesses, then once weaknesses are discovered, further men are used to exploit the situation.

I did also put to him why there are not more dead in a conflict, when for example there are 200 men attacking a fortification defended by 400 men. Surely with the cannon fire, which is followed when the range closes by cannon and musket fire, all the attackers would be killed. Patiently my acquaintance did explain that a cannon is set to lob a missile at a given distance, which the gunner estimates to be the distance from him of the enemy force. However the task is difficult because the enemy force is advancing all the time, and then another factor arises, how fast that force is advancing. The gunner needs judgement to estimate where the enemy force will be when his missile lands. If he gets it right once, there are numerous times when he will get it wrong. It is a similar problem for the musketeer. The range of his weapon is limited and it is not that accurate, and his task is made more difficult when the target is jogging or running towards him. The cannon ball may hit a man and tear his body apart, and its force may even carry it on to hit a man directly behind the first unfortunate fellow. Those on either side usually suffer injuries that prevent them continuing the advance. My acquaintance did also mention the important factor of loading a cannon or a musket. The enemy can cover a great deal of ground while reloading is taking place. In one fight, for example, the Confederate soldiers were advancing at such speed that the Union soldiers could only fire once before they were overwhelmed, and this was repeated several times over with the ranks behind.

I did send Uncle Silas a map of the western theatre of conflict and one of the eastern theatre. Enclosed is a copy of these maps to help you, and to enable you to draw your own conclusion as to the purpose of the military in this conflict between Union and Confederacy.

The politicians do perplex me, and perhaps your greater wisdom in such matters may help me. First, each President does frequently declare he will not be the aggressor, yet both order acts which I can only judge to be aggressive. Secondly, a majority do refer to this as a war, but how can this be so when

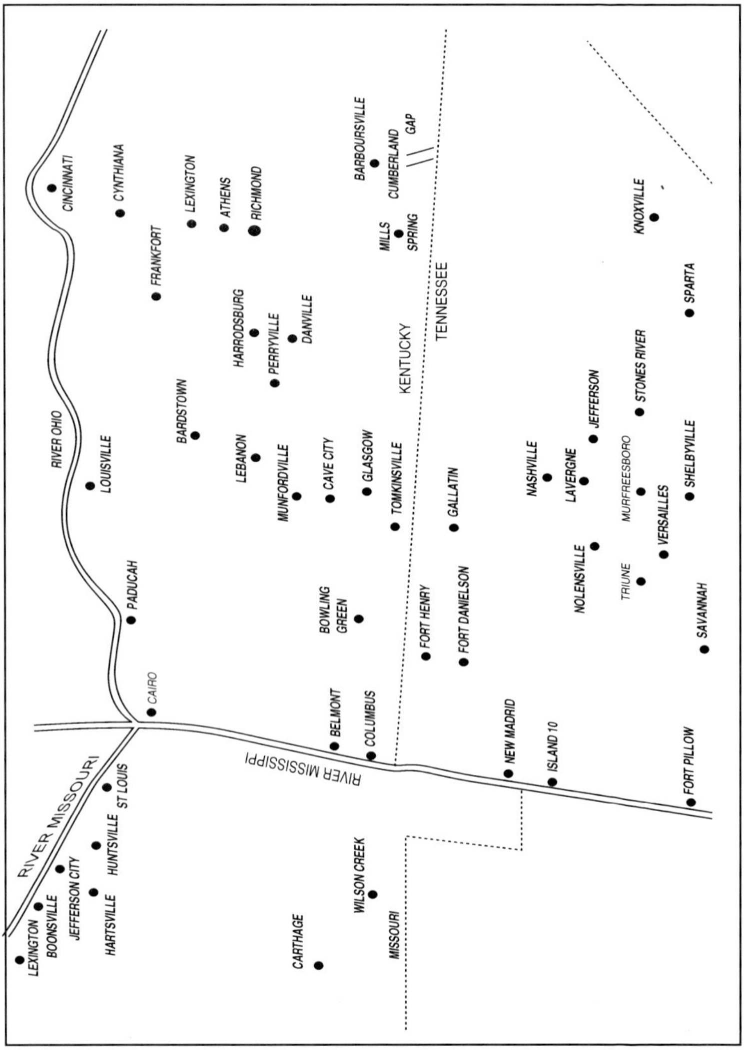
RIVER MISSOURI
RIVER OHIO
RIVER MISSISSIPPI
CINCINNATI
CYNTHIANA
LEXINGTON
ATHENS
RICHMOND
FRANKFORT
HARRODSBURG
PERRYVILLE
DANVILLE
BARBOURSVILLE
CUMBERLAND GAP
MILLS SPRING
KENTUCKY
TENNESSEE
KNOXVILLE
SPARTA
STONES RIVER
JEFFERSON
BARDSTOWN
LOUISVILLE
LEBANON
MUNFORDVILLE
CAVE CITY
GLASGOW
TOMKINSVILLE
GALLATIN
NASHVILLE
LAVERGNE
MURFREESBORO
SHELBYVILLE
VERSAILLES
NOLENSVILLE
TRIUNE
SAVANNAH
PADUCAH
BOWLING GREEN
FORT HENRY
FORT DANIELSON
CAIRO
BELMONT
COLUMBUS
NEW MADRID
ISLAND 10
FORT PILLOW
ST LOUIS
HUNTSVILLE
JEFFERSON CITY
BOONSVILLE
HARTSVILLE
LEXINGTON
CARTHAGE
WILSON CREEK
MISSOURI

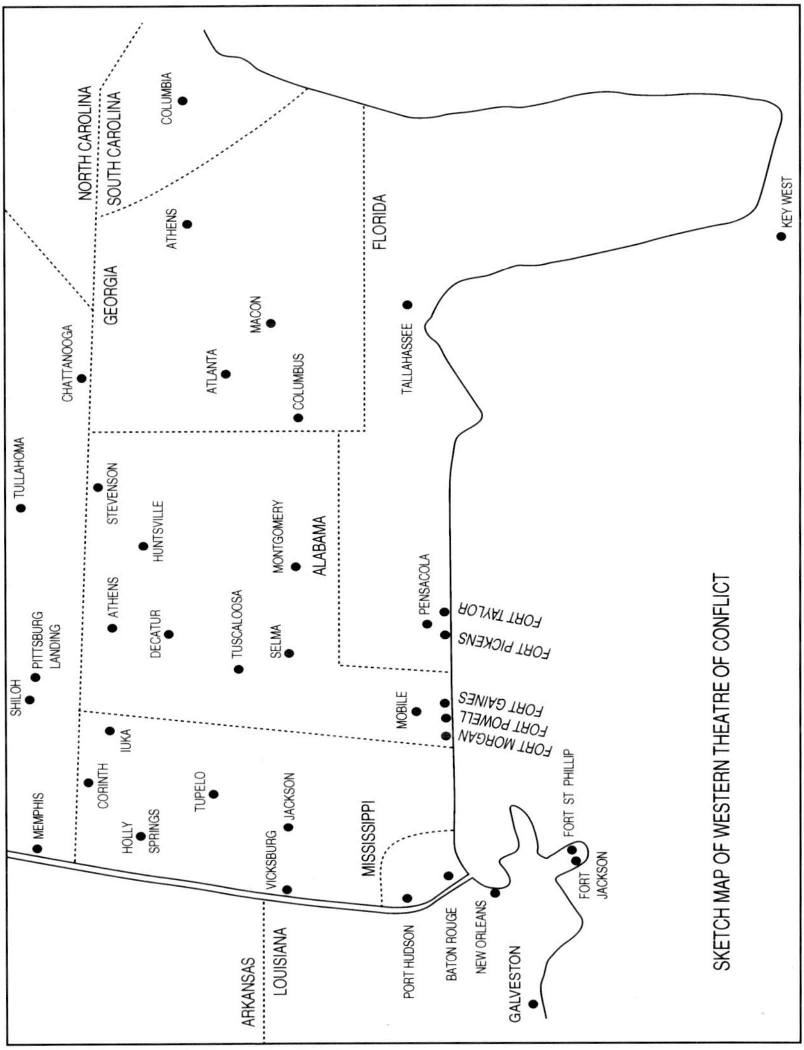

SKETCH MAP OF WESTERN THEATRE OF CONFLICT

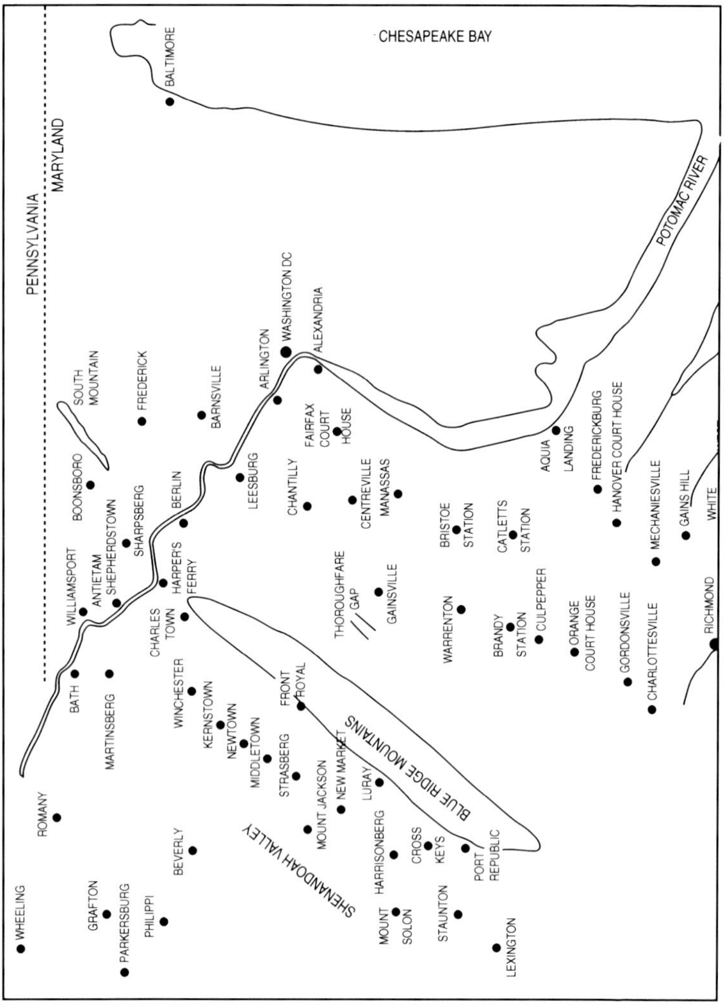
CHESAPEAKE BAY
BALTIMORE
PENNSYLVANIA
MARYLAND
POTOMAC RIVER
WASHINGTON DC
ALEXANDRIA
ARLINGTON
SOUTH MOUNTAIN
FREDERICK
BARNSVILLE
FAIRFAX COURT HOUSE
AQUIA LANDING
FREDERICKSBURG
HANOVER COURT HOUSE
BOONSBORO
LEESBURG
CHANTILLY
CENTREVILLE
MANASSAS
MECHANIESVILLE
GAINS HILL
WHITE
SHARPSBERG
BERLIN
BRISTOE STATION
CATLETTS STATION
WILLIAMSPORT
ANTIETAM
SHEPHERDSTOWN
HARPER'S FERRY
THOROUGHFARE GAP
GAINSVILLE
WARRENTON
CULPEPPER
BRANDY STATION
ORANGE COURT HOUSE
GORDONSVILLE
CHARLOTTESVILLE
RICHMOND
CHARLES TOWN
BATH
MARTINSBERG
WINCHESTER
KERNSTOWN
NEWTOWN
MIDDLETOWN
STRASBERG
FRONT ROYAL
BLUE RIDGE MOUNTAINS
MOUNT JACKSON
NEW MARKET
LURAY
ROMANY
BEVERLY
SHENANDOAH VALLEY
HARRISONBERG
CROSS KEYS
PORT REPUBLIC
WHEELING
GRAFTON
PARKERSBURG
PHILIPPI
MOUNT SOLON
STAUNTON
LEXINGTON

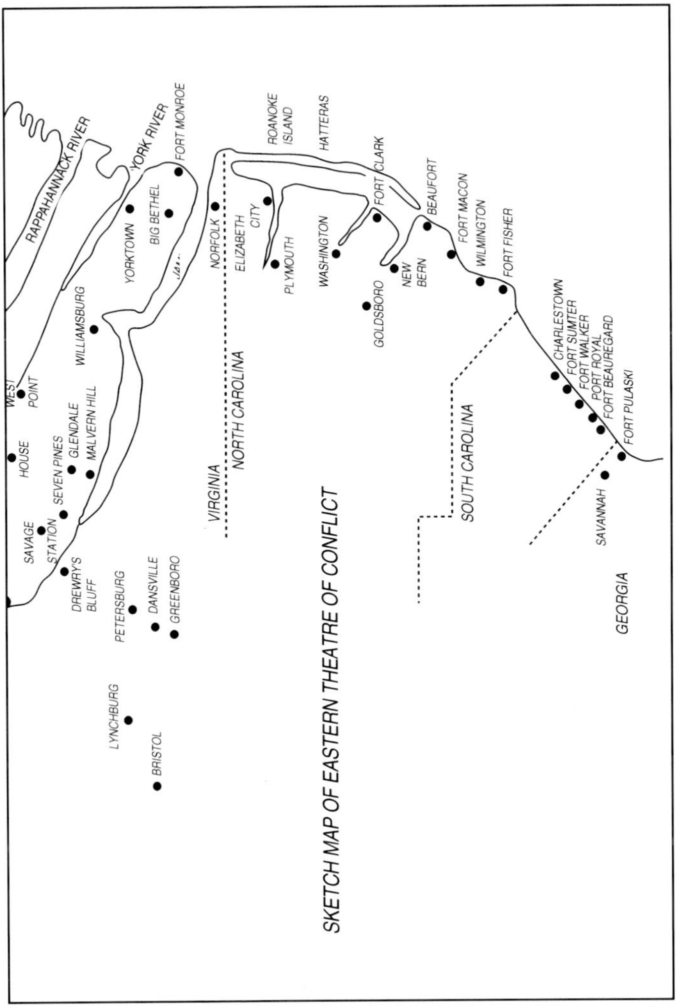

SKETCH MAP OF EASTERN THEATRE OF CONFLICT

the Union does not recognise the Confederacy as a nation, and thus cannot declare war on a nonentity? The Confederacy has its own problem: to gain recognition as a nation. It seems it has yet to prove this to the world. Without nationhood, how can it progress with its objectives? They do say it has yet to prove itself to be worthy of being a nation. President Davis and his government are indeed on the horns of a dilemma.

Sadly, father, the time has run out and I must close this letter, but I promise to write again when I am spared a moment from my work for the company.

I wish you good health and prosperity for 1863.

Your obedient son. . .

Richmond
10 January 1863

My dear mother,

I trust you are well and in good health, and am pleased to say I am well and safe. The demands of the company do not allow me many occasions when I can relax and meditate. It is then my mind wanders back to you and father, and the tranquillity of the family estate. Little did I dream when I left for London that my path of life should lead me to this country. I am indeed grateful to Uncle Silas for having placed his trust in me and sent me here.

How can I describe this country, a term I use in a loose fashion because it appears there are two large factions, each seeking to govern their domain, although one seeks to force the other once again to join with them. In the meantime there is a vast portion of the land that is outside these two major groups.

Yes, mother, I can describe this land as perplexing, and my life, events and changes are sweeping me along apace.

My first image when I landed in New York was how similar in many ways it was to London. It too is cosmopolitan in nature, yet New York is not the seat of government. It is a bustling commercial place with a busy port equal to that of London. But when I ventured beyond the boundaries of New York, I discovered a vastness so unimaginable that even now I cannot fully comprehend it. This land's many and varied conditions do amaze me even after a year of being here, and still I continue to discover new things about the land and the people.

New York seems to be the magnet for those from other lands who seek a new life and hopefully a fortune. Many who come do so to escape oppression and tyranny.

But mother dear, let me tell you of some of the wonders I have encountered. The size of this vast land, for example. Can you possibly imagine that our modest-sized England can be lost in America hundreds of times over? Imagine if you will that you live, for example, in Portsmouth. In England you would be in a populous area, but in America you might need to travel to the Scottish border before you encountered your nearest neighbour. In this land I found communities of Germans, Irish and English, where the cultures and customs of their old country are dominantly expressed throughout their community. To be found elsewhere are segregated religious communities of Puritans and Quakers. To the far west are to be found the original peoples who inhabited this land before the first Europeans set down upon it. These peoples consist of many tribes based on the warrior doctrine.

The first explorers to meet these people described them as being red-skinned, a colour similar to that of the soil in that area, and that is how they became known as Red Indians, although the uncouth use the term redskin in a derogative manner. These people are in fact a collection of many independent communities, each dwelling within its own lands. They are said to understand and commune with nature. Yes, mother, they do have gods, not dissimilar to peoples in other parts of the world where life is dictated by nature. It is an ambition of mine to meet these peoples some time. I do hear their clothes are of exquisite colours and woven designs. I am especially recommended to see their marvellous headdresses which, it is claimed, sweep down their backs to the legs.

Now as to my travels. I did undertake a long and arduous journey by train that took me through many places. Places with the title of city were no larger than an average English village, with dirt roads. People do settle in the strangest of places with hostile terrain, yet they attempt to work the land until nature wins, then the place becomes what is called a Ghost Town, which I understand is eerie to the extreme with all the buildings standing and the wind through them creating the Devil's screams and wails. I believe the Irish have a word for it – banshee. The slow disintegration of these timber buildings reminds me of the ancient ruins of Egypt, Greece and Rome.

Other places, like Montgomery, Vicksburg, Jackson, Columbus, Atlanta and Petersburg each have distinctive characters of their own, and many have well-made roads and footpaths, with churches and distinguished homes and public buildings. I told you of the unexpected, and there is no exception with respect to place names: for example Chattanooga, Tullahoma, Memphis, Wheeling, Boonsville, Centreville and even a Carthage. This to name but a few. In one of my moments of meditation I do wonder how the names came to be. Others of course are easy to identify as being European in origin. Another strange fact is the number of places that end in 'burg' or 'ville'.

A number of places do give themselves the title of city that in my mind do not measure up to the cities I know. Yet Richmond and Washington do not have such a luxury title. Each state boasts its own capital. Imagine that in England: Bristol the capital of the south-west, or Newcastle in the north-east and Liverpool in the north-west.

The people I have met are polite in manners but tend to speak bluntly. I suppose that is because titles of the élite have been left behind in Europe. Here you gain respect for what you are.

Well, mother, time is against me if I am to send this letter on its way to you, so I will wait until next time to relate my journeys by trains, ships, prairie schooners and other means of transport I have experienced. I should also be able to describe some of the places I have visited and the fashions worn by the ladies. Until then, mother dear, I wish you good health, and ask you not to worry about me, because I am safe, and with the help of friends am able to avoid areas of danger.

I am, and remain, your loving son. . .